The Loon Counters

THE
Loon
Counters

Short Stories

Roger Sheffer

Syracuse University Press

Copyright © 2026 by Syracuse University Press
Syracuse, New York 13244-5290

All Rights Reserved

First Edition 2026

26 27 28 29 30 31   6 5 4 3 2 1

For a listing of books published and distributed by Syracuse University Press, visit https://press.syr.edu.

ISBN: 9780815612001 (paperback)
9780815657651 (e-book)

Library of Congress Cataloging-in-Publication Data

Names: Sheffer, Roger author
Title: The loon counters : short stories / Roger Sheffer.
Description: First edition. | Syracuse, New York :
Syracuse University Press, 2026. | Series: New York state series
Identifiers: LCCN 2025033943 (print) | LCCN 2025033944 (ebook) |
ISBN 9780815612001 paperback | ISBN 9780815657651 ebook
Subjects: LCSH: Adirondack Mountains (N.Y.)—Fiction |
LCGFT: Short stories
Classification: LCC PS3569.H392525 L66 2026 (print) |
LCC PS3569.H392525 (ebook) | DDC 813/.54—dc23/eng/20250813
LC record available at https://lccn.loc.gov/2025033943
LC ebook record available at https://lccn.loc.gov/2025033944

The authorized representative in the EU for product safety and compliance is Mare Nostrum Group B.V. Mauritskade 21D, 1091 GC Amsterdam, The Netherlands gpsr@mare-nostrum.co.uk

To my sister Dorothy Fielding

Contents

Acknowledgments

The following people contributed to the existence of this book: my sister, Dorothy Fielding, and her family at Canada Lake; my other siblings—Alison Jurado, Peter Sheffer, Nancy Sheffer, and Jane Salant—with their constant support and encouragement. Former colleagues Rick Robbins, Candace Black, Dick Terrill, and Geoff Herbach, with their continuing interest in my writing. My former student Luke Rolfes, with his intensive and thoughtful feedback. My Minnesota landlord, Tom Hagen, who made a perfect space for creative writing. The people at *Blueline*, especially Donald McNutt, who published so many of my Adirondack stories. Adirondack poet Geri Lipschultz, with her encouraging feedback. Natalia Singer, who guided the reconstruction of this collection, and Laura Fish, always positive. Terry Kinal, church friend and friendly reader. And finally, much thanks to Steve Wilk, a real Adirondack tenor.

The Loon Counters

Torch

February 9, 1980, late afternoon. For exactly one hundred steps, Cheryl LeBeau ran with a stranger, a young man who had already completed five or six miles with the torch. Their feet hit the dry pavement at the same time, as if they had trained for this event together as Olympic teammates. They even breathed together. As they came around a long curve, slightly downhill, Cheryl was thinking of what to say. Something nice about where she lived. For example, by daylight you'd catch the first clear view of Hogback Mountain hanging over the northern horizon, and a green sign saying TOWN OF LOST RIVER, POP. 100, but that was optimistic. The actual population was closer to fifty. And going down. Cheryl said these things to herself, rehearsing, in case a reporter interviewed her.

Winter had begun early, on Halloween, when a pair of loons had to be rescued by boat from a diminishing circle in the middle of Little Silver Lake.

"It's not much," she said.

"What?"

"Nothing," she said.

"Here, you take it now." The young man thrust the torch into Cheryl's insulated mitten. She was surprised by its weight—two pounds, maybe more. It felt lopsided, filled with dangerous fuel. If she tipped it the wrong way, the whole thing might explode, and she would catch fire and run like a torch until she burned up. That would make the local news. Lost River only made the news as the low temperature in the region.

The other runner stayed with her for a while.

"Thanks," Cheryl said.

"I'm beat. Don't drop it. It went through Cooperstown yesterday. Four days from now, it should be in Lake Placid. Something to think about." He laughed and fell back to a walking pace. "It's slipping! Hold it tight." A car honked. Cheryl looked over her shoulder and saw the young man hug someone, probably a girl, possibly his mother. Then he got into a light blue van heading south.

Now she set her own pace. She picked it up slightly, counting, "One and two and three and . . ." until she got to twelve, and started again. The road surface felt good, excellent traction for the middle of winter. She could run like this all the way to Lake Placid—a hundred miles, like the woman who ran across Antarctica. Why not? The roads were clear. But the organizers would stop her at the end of her section, five miles north of here, and she would hand over the torch—to another girl. Melody Anderson. The family had recently moved to the Adirondacks from Utica and had

a year-round place on Silver Lake. A mansion *on the
lake*, according to Melody. "You should see it," she told
Cheryl, though that was the extent of the invitation.

The white Mercedes passed Cheryl, honked twice,
and began to cruise, fifty feet ahead. Melody watched
from the rear window, but it was too dark to see her
clearly. Cheryl thought she was urging her on with
her hands, or putting a hex on her. Their friendship
had not developed the way Cheryl had hoped. They
were school friends, but not confidantes. The problem
might have been the parents—what Melody's parents
thought of Cheryl's father. He had a terrible reputation—as the town drunk. One way to get out from
under such a reputation, for Cheryl, would be to leave
town—on foot, in the dark, downhill all the way.

The diesel exhaust from the car made her cough.
Mrs. Anderson leaned out the window on the passenger side and took Cheryl's picture. She smiled, but
too late, then waved them ahead with her free hand.
They gave her more space, ten car lengths. A northwest wind kicked across an open field and she breathed
more easily. She kept a wad of spearmint gum (three
sticks) tucked inside her cheek, and if she chewed every
few seconds on the count of twelve, the gum would
stay flexible. She loved spearmint.

This was too short a run to have water stations
along the way. And too cold. The water would freeze
in ten seconds. Hot chocolate, though—the people of
her town could have done that much for her.

Two and a half miles until handoff. She felt as if she were running on Mars.

She had trained for the torch relay last fall—three afternoons a week with the high school cross-country team. She should have trained with her right arm held up in the air. She should have pumped iron, picked apples. She should have raised her hand in class more often, conducted the wind ensemble, taken up the violin. Switching the torch over to the left hand didn't help. The left arm was worse. The sleeve was too tight.

Except for the jogging shoes, she looked like a cross-country skier—new parka, knickers, wool cap, wool socks. She should have been on a team, an Olympian—if there had been an ice rink nearby; if the ski area had not shut down, bankrupt, too far from the center of action; if people had cleared cross-country trails and groomed them, instead of snowmobiling to the bars and getting drunk every night.

A guy from Speculator had made the US team. Not cross-country, but close. Biathlon.

At the firehouse, a bunch of locals squatted around a hibachi-type stove, cigarettes dangling from their lips. Cheryl saw the red tips glowing before she picked out the faces attached to them. The men clapped their gloves inaudibly. Harold Shink stood up and yelled, "Go for it, Cher!" He ran out to the road and thumped her on the back. So did her cousin Monty, the crazy high-school dropout.

She tried to say thanks, but her throat was dry. She waved with her free hand. Little Max Biedermann, three years old, whom she often babysat, struggled on his mother's lap, crying. No hat, no mittens, no future.

After another half mile, slightly downhill, the so-called hotel came into view, where, from the front porch, five or six people gawked at Cheryl before turning to go inside, complaining loudly about the extreme cold and how stupid they had been to wait a half hour outside. They might die of the flu. *Just a stupid torch. What's it for? Damned if I know! Whose kid was that? Frank's? No kidding. Where's the no-good bum hanging out now? Old Demarest still letting Frank run up a bar tab?* Cheryl's feet hit the pavement with a detached sound, out of sync with her intended pace and the cadence she was counting. The white moose on the hotel sign flickered, lighting up nearby tree branches. She pictured her father sitting in a dark corner at one of the bars in town. Frank had done nothing but sit and drink and curse since the fire tower closed, permanently. And even before it closed, when he sat up there in the little room all day, watching for fires, he drank. The top of the mountain was littered with broken glass and rusted cans.

Cheryl breathed hard. Her right arm felt like it would crack from holding up the torch. The left arm ached from pumping. But her legs were good. She kept a steady pace and fixed her eyes on the taillights now twenty car lengths ahead of her, as if she might veer off the road without that guidance. As if the road would cease to exist. The torch itself did not illuminate much, although it burned with an acrid stink, and then she thought, *This is a big deal.* Sure, there was another torch—its twin—being carried up to Lake Placid through the eastern Adirondacks. *Harold Shink told me they lit this thing on Mount Olympus in Greece, and that they'd have to fly it all the way back there and send people up that mountain and give it a new flame if I ran off the road and dropped it in the snow just for the hell of it.* He had to be kidding. He was a kidder. The locals could make it the prize in tomorrow's treasure hunt. The treasure was always a gold-painted brick, which could be redeemed for local coupons.

At the next bend, the TEXACO sign wobbled in the breeze, the Christmas lights flickered, meaning, *No snow, no snowmobilers, no business. Our Christmas was so bad we forgot to take down the lights.* Several people sat in parked cars, engines idling and headlights flickering. One honked at her, then several did. *That's nice*, she thought. She slowed to a fast walk. A woman stood in an upstairs window. She did not wave at Cheryl. She was silhouetted, perfectly still, hair like a lampshade. It might have been only a lamp, turned off and backlit.

A car door slammed and Cheryl's mother rushed toward her, uttering gibberish: "Your father went up the goddamn mountain. He's up there in that terrible wind. I told him not to go, but he went anyway."

"No he didn't," Cheryl managed to gasp.

"He told me."

"I have to keep running." She ran in place for a few seconds, afraid her sweat would freeze if she stood still.

"Frank's up there."

"No, Ma," she said. "Frank's in a bar. Demarests. He's lying on the floor in a puddle of vomit. You know that."

"Listen to me!" she screamed. "He went up the mountain more than an hour ago."

"Is he gonna watch me from the tower? Won't see much. You can't see the road from the tower, even with the leaves gone."

"No. He's gonna *burn the tower.* He told me."

She coughed and got back in her car and they all honked at Cheryl, and she rounded the corner and ran through the rock cut, the steepest uphill grade of her run, which she had practiced every day for a month, to get the feel of it. Never on a day quite this cold. Five below. The hard wind chipped at her face.

On the right side of the rock cut, dozens of names were spray-painted, in pairs, but still no name painted next to hers. There never would be, not there. She breathed hard coming up over the high point of the route. The ski area base lodge had once stood a hundred feet from where she was running, the building nothing but an overgrown foundation, next to a jumble of rusted machinery.

Could the fire tower burn? The steps, maybe, and the cabin part on top, which had a wood floor. Dead trees could pick up the blaze if the wind blew hard enough.

The downhill side of Hogback—she slipped on an icy patch, bent her knees, and pretended to be skiing, because running with a torch was not enough of a sport. They didn't hand out medals for torch-running. A publicity stunt, no matter how you looked at it, a way for her hometown and other pathetic little towns on the way to Lake Placid to be part of the Olympics. Cheryl could write about it. Her English teacher had asked for a narrative paper, due next week, about something she had done recently for the first time, and although she had given consideration to the topic of driving a car legally, she decided to write about running the Olympic torch through the town, hoping the paper would not turn out too well because the teacher would make her stand up and read it aloud. Two typed pages would be enough; she would keep it really simple. Five words.

My father burned the tower.

She passed a small parking turnoff. A New York State trail started here and followed the north slope of the mountain to the fire tower. She did not look down for the footprints or snowshoe tracks Frank might have left. She could see the very top of the tower, a small, dark cube. Cheryl imagined the view from there—the miniature torch inching its way around the base of Hogback, blocked by trees for a few seconds, then blazing again. What was Frank thinking as he watched this small ritual connecting their town to the larger world? Did he feel left out? Jealous he hadn't been selected? How could Frank LeBeau have carried the torch? The man lacked the lungs or the heart for it, the style, the balance, the reputation, but Cheryl felt sad for him, that Frank had not lined up with rest of them along the route of the torch-run and cheered when she went by.

Or told her, "Next time, Cher, you'll be on the US Olympic team!"

The wind swirled through the mountain pass. Her teeth felt cold; they were drawing the cold into the rest of her face. The distant taillights of the Mercedes kept her going, no other lights to indicate where she was.

A half-dozen snowmobiles were parked in front of the Klondike. A dozen locals huddled on the porch, cheering and pointing. Cheryl smiled to think of what she represented for them. She slowed to acknowledge their cheers, but the folks on the porch had focused on something further away, higher up, and when she turned around, running in place, she saw what had elicited the cheers—the top of the mountain, lit up, pure gold, flickering in the wind, as if Hogback were Mount Olympus, as if this unremarkable Adirondack mountain, elevation 2,456 feet, were the source of the flame she carried. The sight of the fire on the mountain sucked the breath out of her, made her spit out her spearmint gum, all the juice gone.

She kept running. Someone yelled, "Go!" The Mercedes was now out of sight, the road fading into invisibility. She heard the Klondike people gasping, cheering, a mixture, some of this energy directed at her, she hoped. Frank had gotten the attention he always wanted. How had he done it? He must have carried a gas can all the way, nine hundred feet of glazed rocks and tree roots. Then, at the summit, he had maneuvered up the first flight where the stairs had been ripped out, then doused with gasoline the little enclosed cabin at the top of the tower, fueled by the wood and paper trash that had piled up during the decades. He must have climbed back down, dripping gas on the decayed wooden steps, and lit a match or flipped a Bic.

People might have seen the flame from the top of Whiteface, if the visibility was perfect and anyone bothered to look south from the Whiteface castle. There might be a crowd on Whiteface right then. The Olympics would start in a few days and the place was packed with reporters. People would see it on TV. Someone probably had a TV camera on Whiteface, pointed toward the Hogback fire.

"Give us a panorama. What do you see from the top of the world?"

"Something unusual along the southwest horizon."

"Where would that be?"

"I'm looking at a map. It's the town of Lost River, south of Silver Lake, more than an hour's drive from Lake Placid."

"What is it?"

"Looks like they've lit up an entire mountaintop. Must be having their own Olympics down there."

But no one in Lake Placid would have known where to look. Lost River didn't appear on most maps. It was nothing but a dip in the horizon next to the slight wiggle of an insignificant mountain. Or not even that. The High Peaks south of Whiteface would have blocked any view of the southern Adirondacks.

Cheryl ran backward for twenty steps, her eyes fixed on the Hogback fire. The tower couldn't burn for long, not enough wood, mostly steel. The steel might turn red-hot and glow for a few days. People would come out the following night to see the structure glowing red against the dark sky. The torch-run event hadn't attracted any spectators except locals, not a single tourist along the entire route. And the next day's treasure hunt would make little difference. It might not even happen. Nothing ever did. Fifty permanent residents—just enough to run a torch through Lost River on the way to Silver Lake and beyond.

The taillights of the Mercedes kept her going. She forgot the weight of the torch. The tower fire receded, then disappeared behind a nearby ridge, the atmosphere so thin she couldn't catch even a glow in the sky above where the fire still burned. Two or three cars drove south from Silver Lake, some pulled off along the shoulder, their flashers blinking. The fire reappeared in a notch between two other mountains. Snowy Mountain, possibly.

I can see Snowy, but the opposite direction. Where am I?

The Mercedes pulled over and Melody sprang out from the back seat and started jogging in place. Rich girl. She had Day-Glo stripes on her running shoes. Lemon yellow.

"What are you looking at?" Melody asked.

"The fire," Cheryl said.

"We can't stop," she said. "We have to keep running."

"Why can't we stop?"

"The torch."

"What? You think it will go out if I stop?"

"Don't tip it like that!"

"I'm sorry," Cheryl said. "My brain is freezing."

"People up north are waiting for this," Melody said, reaching with her yellow mitten. "There's a strict schedule. Silver Lake. A bunch of people are waiting in the freezing cold up there, in front of Olmstead's. It's below zero now and we're late."

"They're sitting in nice, warm cars. Like yours." Cheryl nodded toward the Mercedes.

"The other torch will get to Lake Placid before we do."

"By a few seconds, right?" She handed the torch to Melody and kept her hands on it long enough to be sure Melody had a good grip. She ran with her until her breath was gone, another quarter mile. No conversation.

"Good-bye, Melody."

Melody said nothing. Cheryl shook the pain out of her arms, bent over and massaged her calves—alone on the highway, watching the Mercedes disappear into the dark as it kept pace with Melody and her lemon-yellow feet. With the torch no longer in her hands, Cheryl felt absolutely cold, unplugged from any source of energy. She could barely stand. Her legs were cramping.

The highway curved north and west and north again, and the light kept moving, mile by mile, toward Lake Placid. Cheryl felt disconnected from history. Her hands were dead. Better hands would carry the torch the last few miles, the last few yards, probably a gold medalist from decades ago. Huge crowds would cheer. And they would have the flame up there in Lake Placid for a couple weeks, then douse it. Put a lid on it or something. Other flames would go out. Hogback Mountain would cool down. People would forget what her father had done, forget him forever, scratch his name from the record books. It was just an old wrecked tower, no longer in use, all of its steps burned. The state would tear it down.

Torch: She knew another history. Long ago (she had read in a book) the best mountaintops in the Adirondacks had been burnt over, struck by lightning, eroded to bare rock. Perfect views. In the old days, a hundred years ago, it would have been beautiful—the top of a mountain on fire, no way to put it out.

Torch: She flexed her empty hand.

She began the return walk, thinking about nothing beyond how to work the cramps out of her calves and how her feet touched the pavement. No slipping. Her heart thumped solid and steady, as if she had been hooked up to a new source of energy. Her hands felt warm now. She jogged a hundred yards, accelerated, found a comfortable speed. She thought of the next place to hold the Winter Olympics, a faraway country with a weird name. She decided that she would train for the cross-country ski team, if it only meant running this stretch of highway, back and forth, the next three years, over and over and over. Alone, nothing in her hand. Ice, snow. Whatever the conditions. She would run the damn thing every day, even the hottest day of summer, when even these tiny remnants of snow would be just a dim blur in the back of her mind and she would long for the cold air that she now breathed.

Silver Creek

Late August, late twentieth century. Three women—Joan DeWitt and two of her many cousins—were enjoying a short hike on the yellow-marked trail that connected the hamlet of Silver Lake with the Northville-Placid Trail. They always turned around at the waterfall, where cell coverage ended. Hiking any further entailed risks.

"Joan, you're moving too fast," Carolyn said.

"You need better boots," Joan said.

"You always say that," Emma said. She was Carolyn's daughter, a second cousin once removed. Neither cousin had a camp in the Adirondacks; they lived in side-by-side townhouses outside the Blue Line—in Herkimer, close enough to make day trips, for day hikes. The three women hiked the Yellow Trail (as it was known locally) every Saturday during the summer, weather permitting. *Walked* would be the more appropriate verb, as the trail was flat and manicured. Joan's comment about better boots was facetious; they could have been walking in flip-flops. Or barefoot. Occasionally, they would meet actual long-distance hikers headed west toward the Silver Lake store to buy provisions, a three-mile walk from the N-P Trail junction—where the state should have put a sign saying that hot dogs and ice cream cones were available an hour away. The three cousins never got as far as the junction, although Joan would have liked to. Unlike her cousins, she was adventurous.

One morning on the Yellow Trail, they were caught in the rain, a mile from the store. No umbrellas, no hats. Emma said, "I could be home on my treadmill." Her mother said, "You never use it, except to hang your laundry." But Emma continued, "If all I wanted was the exercise, I could be on my treadmill, looking at the beautiful scenery on the screen. Yosemite, Grand Canyon." No Adirondacks.

Their usual turnaround had a wide log (actually, a fallen hemlock, branchless) where the women would sit and look at Silver Creek, listen to the two-foot-high waterfall. But not this time. A man was sitting on the log, head tipped back, eyes closed. Blue seed cap, big nose, turkey neck, red plaid shirt.

Joan knew him. "Hello, Harold."

"I was hoping to disappear," he said.

"You're very visible," Joan said. Her cousins laughed, though she had not intended to make fun of Harold. She knew his story, told to her in short chapters by Robert, her writing-group friend who was trying to turn Harold into a fictional character. Harold Shink was Robert's handyman and caretaker. A man who was happy only when away from his home, taking care of other people's property. He didn't feel safe around his own kids. One time—he told Robert—he awoke in the middle of the night to discover his oldest son trying to strangle him, bare-handed.

Harold opened his eyes. "Ladies," he said, nodding at them.

"Why would you want to disappear?" Emma asked in her high, sweet voice. "You're in a beautiful place right now."

"That's true," he said. He stood up, turned around, and briefly glanced at the waterfall, squinting, as if it might blind him. "You know, a long time ago, before they built this trail, we would bushwhack out here, just to listen to the falls. My youngest daughter and me. Tammy. Boy, that was ancient history. I named this waterfall for her, Tammy Falls, and she looked at me and said, 'Papa, it's only two feet high. Can't you find a bigger one for me?' What do you think of that? She was only seven years old."

"I never met her," Joan said.

"She'd be thirty now," Harold said.

"Oh," Joan's cousins said in unison. Joan knew the story of Tammy's death, told to her, of course, by Robert—three teenagers in the car, an icy road north of Silver Lake, a curve around the base of the mountain. Harold had been one of the volunteers in the fire engine arriving at the scene. That Harold could talk about his daughter, even years later, was remarkable.

"I'm at peace when I sit here. I still hear her voice, asking for a better waterfall."

"You haven't disappeared," Joan said.

"Not this time," he said. "I'm not equipped."

"Oh?"

Harold swept the pine needles from his sap-stained khaki pants, examined his rough hands. The tip of one pinky was missing. Missing fingers, missing teeth—not unusual in this part of New York State. "Next time," he said. "It could be soon. Life is hard. Next time, I'll load up my Kelty pack and head out on this trail and only stop here to rest and take one last look at Tammy Falls. Then, east and northeast. Wilderness forever. You know, beyond the East Branch?"

"We always turn around here," Emma said. "We *don't* know."

"East branch of what?" Carolyn said.

"Sit down, ladies," Harold said. "This might take a while." They sat on the log and watched Harold deliver a speech. He grabbed the trunk of a maple sapling and held on tight as he spoke about what lay to the east and northeast, one of the great wilderness tracts in the Adirondack Park. The Yellow Trail joined the N-P Trail, shared it for a mile, then "shot off" into the deeper woods, toward a beautiful lake that few people—even locals—knew about, where a hermit named Joshua lived, and a family of loons. Harold hoped Joshua was still living, because he needed to find him and talk to him again. Harold had discovered Joshua decades ago, after being lost for three days and surviving on stream water and bugs—evidently, a failed attempt to escape from his miserable family. "I won't get into the gory details," he told the women, who were hanging on every word.

"Keep talking," Joan said. "This is all new to me."

"If alive, he could be a hundred," Harold said. "Or ninety. A shy man, like most hermits. I don't want nobody going in there with helicopters and TV cameras or nothing like that. The last of the great hermits." They all laughed. "The creek is laughing, too," Harold said. So Joshua had saved Harold's life, fed him, dried his clothes over a fire, kept him out of the rain, and guided him out of the wilderness the next day. "Tried to put me on the right path, if you know what I mean."

"Literally," Joan said, as she thought about Harold's future *right path*, whether the Yellow Trail and beyond would be that path. She was not one to give advice to her elders, even the most misguided of them. It was the same cliché an advisor had used when Joan was young, her first year of college, and making bad choices. *You need to find the right path*, the advisor had said. Joan had taken the advice and started hiking the next day.

"The right path," Harold repeated, touching the brim of his seed cap. "And that was just about the extent of it. The path got me home, and my wife smelled the smoke on my clothes and began to yell at me."

"You were innocent," Emma said.

"Things only got worse, which you all probably know about. So, you might say I'm about to walk away from my problems, literally."

Harold's understanding of his situation was quite re-markable, the women agreed over coffee and scones at the Silver Lake store picnic table, where they typically shared their observations after their Saturday morning hike.

That Harold never did strap on his Kelty pack and literally walk away from his problems was considered unremarkable. That he died a few years later—in a local bar's parking lot after a fistfight with his oldest son—was also considered unremarkable, though tragic. The women didn't want to talk about it. They were thinking about the paths they had walked, paths not nearly as simple or clear as the one that followed Silver Creek to the waterfall. Flat, unobstructed, well-marked—a corrective, therapeutic. *Therapeutic* was the word Joan had once used in front of Carolyn and Emma, which made them laugh, though it was a nervous laugh, implying some truth. In Joan's opinion, both cousins needed hiking therapy—not just because of the fights with the men in their lives, but because of their frequently described "fears." A fear of the wilderness, of who might be lurking there. One time, as they sat on their favorite log, Emma said, "What if we hike another mile into the wilderness and here comes my old boyfriend around the corner, barreling down the path, brandishing a knife?" At the time Joan thought, *That could never happen. We're safe.*

North of Cooperstown

Late July, 1993. Max Biedermann pulled tight on the yellow string and threw the last bundle against the beer cooler—unsold newspapers from a rainy weekend. On a shelf behind the cash register his boss Diane Olmstead had stacked the unreturnable papers—reserves, with names written in green ink. She would bill customers for their papers whether they picked them up or not. On the bottom of the pile Max found a *New York Times* more than two weeks old, the name JOAN written across the top.

Customers got mad when things weren't done a certain way. "You're pretty young to be working," they would say to Max.

"I'm sixteen," he would answer. "Almost seventeen."

They kept score. When they asked for their papers, he might forget their names. One woman knew exactly how many times he had forgotten. "I'm way ahead of you so far this summer," she would say. "Seven to one."

Diane kept score on whether he washed his hands before working at the deli counter. She also notched a stick on the wall behind the deli whenever he weighed out "the perfect pound" of hamburger, three times already since Memorial Day. When his many attributes had been properly measured—in other words, "scored"—the general public would finally know that Max was a good guy, a hard worker, that he never cheated in school, that he kept his promises and told the truth even when to do so would result in a material loss. He always paid for the pints of milk he took from the cooler, the black-and-white cookies, the slices of sharp cheddar cheese so light they hardly registered on the scale.

He opened Joan's reserved paper to check the sports page. The Red Sox were on a streak, the Yankees in a slump. The Hall of Fame classic would be played on August 2 in Cooperstown. He flipped to the editorial page. Someone in Connecticut wrote a letter condemning a politician for his "dictatorial" control of the Adirondack Park. The State of New York needed money to buy more wilderness land before it was all turned into subdivisions. This didn't mean a lot to Max—there were no subdivisions near Silver Lake in any direction, though he'd seen plenty of FOR SALE signs along the road, the same signs year after year. He lived with his mother in a double-wide mobile home a mile south of Silver Lake, on two acres of uneven land fronting the main highway. Technically, they lived in Lost River. If you told people you lived in Silver Lake, they might assume you lived right *on* the lake.

A back-page article estimated that there were only a hundred nesting pairs of loons in the entire

Adirondacks. Max knew of at least two pairs on Silver Lake.

The business section of the *Times* had nothing but numbers until he got to the last page, where several obituaries were crowded together. Men in their eight-ies. In their photos they looked much younger, with dark hair and bright eyes. The photos had been taken a long time ago—1953, 1960, 1963. Below a photo taken in 1963, a dark-haired guy in a baseball uniform had smiled for the photographer.

John Gerling, 81, Played Third Base for Dodgers

Max had to take away the hair and the teeth before he could make sense of the story. Turn John into Jack and then Cracker Jack. Attach a skinny body to the head, give it a limp, put it in an ancient Chevy pickup, have it drive up to the store porch on a Sunday morn-ing, honk twice, then call out in a yodel, "Hey paper boy, gimme one of them O-D's, and put it on my bill." O-D was short for the *Utica Observer-Dispatch.* Then Cracker Jack would say, "How about one of them rot-ten apples she's selling. She oughta *give* 'em away. Why don't you just pitch me a red one, not too bruised." But Max would never pitch it to him. He would walk up to the truck window and hand the apple to Cracker Jack, and the old man would shake his head, disappointed.

Or Jack would say, "Fill 'er up, boy. With no-lead." He would pronounce *lead* as in "lead-off batter."

Olmsteads didn't sell anything *but* no-lead, premium or regular. Jack preferred regular.

Max was only twelve then, his store duties mainly to sell the papers on the porch Sunday mornings, bag ice, sort the returnable bottles and cans. Couldn't sell beer, couldn't run the slicer—too young. On slow days he raked the beach and ran messages between the store and dock. Or he'd pump gas for the customers who didn't want their hands to smell like gasoline or were too fat or crippled to get out of their car. They usually tipped him.

He read the obituary:

> John Gerling died in Bassett Hospital, Coopers-town, New York, after a long illness. A native of the Town of Lost River, a remote Adirondack hamlet eighty miles north of Cooperstown, Ger-ling owned a small wilderness hotel north of there, and was an experienced backwoods guide. Known more for his fielding skills than his strength as a batter, he played one hundred straight games with-out making an error during the 1948 season.

Max knew all the stats. By 1963, Cracker Jack was a de-cade past retirement. What was he doing in a baseball uniform? And what had made him smile? It might have been the memory of the hundred-game streak, the idea that other people still remembered it and might, in the future, write about it. Or the photographer had told him to smile: "You need to look good when they print your obituary." By the time Max knew him, Jack had changed—lost his hair, the shine in his face, the ability to stand up straight.

"Can I buy this paper?" Max asked Diane.

"What would you want with an old *New York Times*?" She lit up a cigarette. She hardly ever smoked inside the store. "Or a new one, for that matter?"

"I can read," he said, his voice cracking. "I'll pay full price."

She stubbed out her cigarette and grabbed the paper from him. "I already put this on her bill. Joan DeWitt. She's a piece of work."

"Really?"

"When Cousin Joan comes up from the city next week—"

"Cousin?"

"It's complicated. We're all related. When she comes up next week, I'll hand several months' worth over to her. She does the puzzle, you know. What she buys it for. Nothing else. Sits in her fancy tent and does puzzles until dark."

"Doesn't read the news?"

"Nope. She tells me the rest of the paper is worthless and I should cut out the crossword puzzles for her, save her the bother. When I tell her it will cost an additional two bucks for my labor—per puzzle—she says, go ahead, put it on my bill. But I was only kidding. I don't have time to cut out the puzzles for her."

"I do."

"Next thing you know, people will ask me to cut out the box scores of their favorite baseball teams

because it's all they care about. You and your Yankees."
She kicked the last bundle to the edge of the porch.
She frowned, as if in pain.

"I could do that," he said. "Two bucks apiece."

She laughed. Her laugh was like a cough. Diane
wasn't really old, maybe thirty, but suffered from many
medical problems, possibly caused by her extreme
weight. Max guessed that she weighed over three hundred pounds, but it wasn't a number that would be
written down anywhere (like, scribbled on the wall),
or that anyone dared to talk about.

Later, when Diane went out to greet the Freihofer
bread truck, donut in hand, Max took a pair of scis-
sors and cut out Cracker Jack's obituary from Joan De-
Witt's paper, checking first to make sure the puzzle
wasn't on the other side. Then he folded the clipping
in his pants pocket. It didn't take up much room in
there. He'd done something he might have to lie about.

Four years earlier Max, then twelve years old, had been
tossing rocks into the sandbank, a mile off the lake on
Gussey Road. He would have played catch with another kid, but there weren't any kids his age in the town
of Lost River—or Silver Lake except in summer—and
he would have preferred a real ball, but didn't own one.
Didn't own a proper glove, either. He would pick out
specific clumps of grass near the base of the sandbank
and aim hardball-size rocks at them, keeping track of
hits and misses by gouging marks in the ground with
his bootheel.

A vehicle approached, gears grinding, tailpipe clanking on the potholed road. Thinking it might be an older kid he didn't like, Max looked for a hiding place, but the sandbank didn't offer much to hide behind, only a few scrawny hemlock trees. So he sat on a rock and pretended to rest from a hike or something.

Turned out to be Jack's truck. Cracker Jack. He honked the farty horn, his window already rolled down so he could yell at Max to toss him a rotten apple.

"Whatcha doing, boy?"

"Resting."

"You're seventy years too young for that. Get busy!"

"Get busy?"

Jack spat a mouthful of dark stuff into the high grass, a nice long arc that traveled twenty feet. "With whatever hard work you were resting from."

"I was tossing rocks. I didn't break anything."

"Show me."

Max picked up a fist-size rock, gripped it between his thumb and first two fingers, and pitched it into the sandbank.

Cracker Jack laughed. "You were resting from *that?*" He opened the door and stepped down from his truck, wincing when his left foot hit the ground. "My other foot, you know, I don't feel at all," he said. "Luckily." He walked with the assistance of a twisted wooden cane.

Max stood up. "You can sit on my rock."

"Cheap seats?"

"Free," Max said as he stepped to the side.

"I'm not sitting today. Can't sit. Lord, what sitting will do to ya!" So he stood and stared. "You got a ball and glove?"

"Nope."

"Why not?"

"No money," Max said softly.

"You work for Diane whatever-her-last-name-is. Don't she pay you nothing?"

"I give it all to my mom," he said.

"You want one?" Jack asked. "I mean, two. I mean both. Hell, I can't talk." He whistled and kind of zipped one finger in front of his mouth while his cane fell to the ground. "You want a ball and a glove?"

"I don't know, maybe." Of course he did, but no one ever gave him anything and he didn't know how to react. He picked up the fallen cane and handed it to Jack.

"C'mon, boy, get in the truck."

He hesitated.

"I said, get in the truck. What could an old cripple like me do to you, besides bore you to death?"

They headed north on the Cedar Lake Road, past where the power lines ended, with no flat places except the road itself. Max had never gone up that way. No reason to. It was a resort area with campsites and canoe routes and bird watchers. The only direction he and his mother ever went was south, to the county seat, to shop for groceries and deal with Social Services. Not much scenery along the way, just a couple of scummy lakes and burnt-out businesses, an abandoned church, a few shacks and trailers.

Going north, you'd see more pine trees and swamps and sometimes a mountain with a steep rock face, and, every few miles, a quick turnoff with a sign for a wilderness trail.

"You never been to my hotel," Jack said.

"I'm not allowed to drink."

"Big deal." Jack laughed. "I'm not either."

"You're not?"

"The boss says so."

"The boss?"

"Oh, he's just my little brother." Jack belched and pursed his lips, to keep another belch from coming out. "You never seen him, I know, because he's in even worse shape than me. Everybody thinks he's dead."

"You're in great shape," Max said.

"The hell I am. I'm a walking corpse."

Off the grid, beyond the last utility pole, people in the occasional log cabin might keep a gas-powered generator chugging in back, tanks of propane they would pick up at the store. "Would you lift that thing for me, boy?" they would say. The highway curved around the oxbow of some peaceful river, and Max could see across the marsh all the way to a rock face that shot up vertically from the floor of the valley, then rounded off in a dark green top.

"Pretty scenery," Jack said. "The main reason I came home after I retired. And it's cheap. Cheap as it gets. Free."

They turned left and followed an unmarked road that quickly changed over to gravel, hardly one lane. Jack didn't bother to watch the road as he talked to Max, gesturing with his hands, steering with his knees. Somehow he aimed the truck so it missed the worst boulders and potholes. "It's all state land," he said. "Except our five little acres they wanna buy from us." After two miles on this wilderness road, Jack honked twice, then turned right into a gravel driveway. "If I don't toot the horn, the boss gets nervous about the sound of a car. He's always yappin' about the criminals driving into the Adirondacks. He lies in bed all day thinking about it, the prison escapees headed down this way."

A yellow sign nailed into the side of the dark green, tar-papered building read,

HOME PLATE. GOOD FOOD. ROOMS. HUNTERS WELCOME.

"You eat yet today?" Jack asked as they got out of the truck.

"Of course." Trix for breakfast, a Snickers bar for lunch, a few scraps of bologna from the meat slicer, all paid for.

"I'm chief cook and bottle washer lately. Last ten years, matter of fact. So I thought I'd ask. This ain't the weekend. Dining room's closed, but we could sneak a few slices of cold venison from the kitchen. The deer's still standing in the walk-in cooler, skinned and ready to be sliced."

"I'm not hungry."

Once inside, they stood in a kind of lobby, with a saggy green couch, a small bookcase, a couple of deer heads staring at each other from opposite walls, and various items displayed in crooked picture frames—photos and news clippings. Some of the stories concerned Jack Gerling, faded clippings from a defunct local paper that bragged about his Major League exploits. Others concerned Don Gerling, his high school games, the amazing speed of his pitches, so fast they were invisible, one article said. Don must have been Jack's little brother. *The boss.* Everything in the hotel was old, wrinkled, falling.

The place smelled like ashes and urine.

Jack led him down a hallway past a door that Max peeked in without stopping and saw a very old man lying under blankets, breathing heavily, his bald head turned away. "Don't worry," Jack said. "He knows we're here. He's listening to every damn word we say." He tapped on the doorframe with his twisted cane and moved on.

At the far end of the hall was a closet full of equipment—pack baskets, snowshoes, fishing gear—all of it very obsolete-looking and not in good condition.

"The museum," Jack said.

"Really?"

"I like to call it 'the museum.'" He cleared his throat. "Since I couldn't get in the other one."

"The other one?"

"Never mind. Boss don't wanna hear about it, tired of my whining." He rubbed his hands together, a baseball gesture, like what you'd do before you picked up a bat so it wouldn't slip when you swung it.

"Don't you use any of this stuff? Or your kids?"

"Zero kids that I know of," Jack said.

Max had no idea what he meant.

"No wife neither, since 1951, which was when I came back to Lost River to take care of baby brother. Wife couldn't stand the cold, the isolation. So she dumped me, took off in the middle of the night." Wood shelves went up higher than Jack could reach. "Bring me a chair from out in the hall," he said to Max, who brought it over quickly. "Better keep close by in case I fall on my ass." Jack stood on the chair, precariously, one-legged, and slid a shallow wooden box from the top shelf.

"What's that?"

"I guess I keep this junk up here because it don't mean nothing to me no more. It's not like I'm afraid of thieves."

There were brass plaques and triangular felt flags and a couple of leather mitts and several hardballs rolling around. "What you need is a decent ball and glove," Jack said. "Hell of a lot better than a rock and a bunch of sand. Poor as we were in those days, me and my brother never used a rock. We got more equipment in here than *we'll* ever need. Been years since Don and me played pitch and catch. Decades."

Max could not imagine where the brothers played. Home Plate had no open space around it, nothing but trees and swamp. If there had ever been a baseball diamond, it had overgrown, like the one behind the old post office in Lost River, where Max's deceased father had supposedly played.

"Don was the pitcher. Fastball, slider. I could never catch what he threw so I'd just hold up a piece of wood and block it. Here, take this and try it on. Don's old glove from high school. He won't mind." The glove, way too large, slipped off Max's left hand and fell on the floor.

"I'm sorry." He picked up the glove and tucked it under his arm.

"It didn't break into little pieces, did it?"

"Nope."

"Then I won't call the sheriff," Jack said. "The cow that died to make that glove, she don't care neither. She died in 1930. You can keep it for when you're older."

"Thanks."

"But this ball here should fit in your hand right now, nice and cozy." He handed it to Max. "Be gentle with it."

"You played baseball." It seemed like the dumbest thing to say.

"Yeah, a little, wasn't nothin' to write home about. The boss, he was the one with all the talent, but when they scouted him, right after the war, he didn't go. *Wouldn't* go. They had two big-shot scouts from the Yankees drove up here in a fancy car to watch him pitch, shaking their heads at how good he was. Invisible pitches, almost like he'd faked it, like those knife throwers at the carnival. You know what I mean?"

"Yup."

"Yankees mailed him a bus ticket, train ticket. Don wouldn't go. Too homesick. Seventeen years old. You should of seen him fightin' with Mom, her telling him to get his ass out the door, out of the Adirondacks, and Don crying and saying he couldn't do it. It's okay, I don't care if he hears me. Then he got called up for military service, Korean War, and being homesick didn't keep him out, though I wish it had. The war nearly killed him. We're seven years apart in age. I was already too old to be drafted, too flat-footed. I kept playing."

Max looked at the ball Jack had given him. "You played for the Dodgers."

"Hell, they're never gonna put me in the Hall of Fame, if you wanted to know. They'll wait until I'm dead."

"I don't play much myself, but I want to."

"They wait until you're dead. But if you die and they don't vote you in right away, then forget it, unless your friends keep trying. Home Plate is eighty miles north of Cooperstown, but the way I see it, it's more like a million."

Max shook his head.

"Look at the names on your ball," Jack said. "It's *your* ball now, okay?"

"Okay."

"Those are real autographs, in real ink. 1951. Roy Campanella, Duke Snider, Jackie Robinson, Gil Hodges. Don't rub those off now." Jack's name was on there, too, written smaller than the others, but neat and steady, very official. *John Gerling*.

"I won't."

"If you have to write over the autograph because it started to disappear, then it's not the real autograph anymore."

"What if the groove is still there, and the ink kind of flows into it?"

"Then we'd bring in the ump to make the call."

"Your brother?"

"No," Jack laughed. "He's blind."

They walked past the open door. The raspy breathing had become smoother. Jack closed the door, carefully. "He's heard enough," he said. "You have a brother?"

"Nope. Zero brothers."

"Take care of that ball," he said to Max, then drove him home. For the entire ten miles Max kept thinking, *Maybe Cracker Jack wants to play pitch and catch with me. I should ask him, although if he really wanted something, wouldn't he just say so? He's out of shape, could be the reason. He could sit while we played. I wouldn't throw it too hard. I'd try not to hit him. He could check out my style and tell me how to improve.* Max moved his lips, even began to mumble these things, but when Jack said, "What the hell are you talking about?" he answered, "Oh nothing." They would ruin the ball if they played pitch and catch with it. The names would disappear.

When school started in September, Max didn't bring the ball to show his friends. It could have gotten stolen, or some other kid might touch Jack's name and make it disappear. He kept the ball in the closet, on a high shelf next to the too-large glove, while he waited for his hand to grow.

When Max unfolded the obituary from his pants pocket and showed it to his mother, she frowned and said, "The end to a sad story," and then clammed up, turned on the TV, and wouldn't talk to him the rest of the afternoon. The end? He reread the obituary. There were no survivors, no family mentioned. *No kids that he knew of.* Max kept thinking about the brother, Don Gerling, who probably had no story written about him when he died, certainly no picture in a baseball uniform, no nickname—like, "He was known to his brother as 'The Boss.'"

At work the next day, Max searched for Jack's charge book, among the *G*'s. His old friend might have died without paying his debts.

"What are you looking for?" Diane asked.

"Jack Gerling. Cracker Jack."

"He died a month ago, down in Cooperstown."

"I just wondered if his old charge book was still sitting here in the rack."

"Are your hands clean?"

"Yup. Cracker Jack, he used to drive here in the old pickup, you know, and I'd pump gas for him, or run in and get his six-pack of Genny Cream Ale, remember?"

"Yeah. A long time ago, Max."

"Well, he'd charge it, right?"

"That was back when I was an amateur at this," she said, quickly writing names on the reserved papers, not paying attention to what she was doing. "I used to let them charge their gas and their beer. I learned my lesson."

"What happened to Jack's charge book?"

"I still got it upstairs in the file cabinet. He owes me five hundred dollars. I'd be lucky to get half of it."

"But he's dead."

"Oh, I'll get the money out of him somehow."

"He never paid?"

"Started out making regular payments," she said, nibbling on a light brown cookie. "Back in the old days, before you were born, when my parents ran the place. He'd pay monthly—ten or twenty bucks, brand-new crisp bills. It never covered the balance."

"He was poor?"

"Who knows? Maybe he was rich. I got rich people who owe me money, too. A lot of these deadbeats are millionaires." She waved toward the rack of charge books, cookie still in hand, crumbs falling. "I don't know much about Jack. A character, is what the locals said. A *character*. It means, you can't trust them. They're hiding a *big secret*."

"I liked him."

"Well, he stopped coming to the store. I suppose he drove into town for provisions after I told him to pay up. Which is what they do. You see them driving along the highway, top speed, never mind the speed limit."

"He played ball in the Major Leagues."

"Zoom, zoom, zoom, all I see is their exhaust. They never show their guilty faces."

"Did you ever meet his brother?"

"The brother died a long time ago, is what I heard," she said, turning away from Max, finishing the cookie. "A relief. All I have to say."

Max's mother was always telling him to throw things away. She'd say, "Get busy. Clean your room. We're moving out of this dump next week." And he used to believe it. But they never moved. They stayed in Lost River, off the lake in the double-wide, and his mother had him shop in Olmsteads's store for milk and bread, cash only. She didn't get out much. When her car died, she pretty much stayed at home with the TV on all day. She didn't have the strength to clean up after him, to take his junk and haul it to the side of the road. She could only talk about it, make him feel as if everything he owned was worthless. *It's nothing but junk!* In his closet he kept a cardboard box full of it. And the shelf of the closet—things were packed tight in there. If you tried to pull one thing out of the mess, another thing would drop on your head.

He had a *signed Major League ball* up there, and a professional glove that might fit his hand now. He did not need a chair to retrieve these items; he'd grown a few inches. The glove was soft, like flesh, the flesh of an old man, a mummy. The ball, still hard, usable. He brought them down and inspected them. The ball smelled like grass, kind of refreshing, but the glove smelled like it had rotted. In fact, the leather was wet, and Max wondered if rain had come through a crack in the ceiling, from a hole in the roof. He stuck the rotten glove in a paper bag and considered throwing it in the garbage.

Then he carried the glove—and the ball—out the door. He followed the shortcut path to the sandbank, now overgrown.

"So," he said to himself, "did they bury him in Cooperstown, or up here in the Adirondacks?"

He felt the ball in his shorts pocket, hard against his hip, and swung the rotten glove in the paper bag, twisting the neck of the bag.

Eighty miles north of Cooperstown. Did they have a funeral for Cracker Jack? Who would "they" be? The brother had already died. No one still in town would think about him. The land might have been sold to a developer to pay his debts. Or the state had finally bought it and torn down Home Plate. Buried it.

The shortcut trail crossed over a ridge. In a clearing, a cloud of little bugs attacked him. He swung at them with the paper bag. The ball stayed in his pocket. He touched the pocket, to make sure.

"Take that!"

The sandbank had stayed the same over the past few years. People wrote their names in the hard sand, since all the suitable rock faces were used up. One good storm would wash the letters away. In the flat area below was a small fire pit and a few charred logs, evidence that people camped here. A Genesee beer can, then another, both rusted. Kids partied here, mostly summer kids. Max never did. He kicked at the loose soil to make a hole, then dug at it with a stick for a while. He dropped the old glove into the hole. It looked like a mummified hand or the amputated hand of a giant, from a time before Max's birth, when real giants played the game. *Like . . . Mel Ott.* When they stopped playing ball they shrank to normal size, went to bed, turned their heads to face a blank wall. Or they became "characters," as Diane had said. Characters with big secrets.

Max covered the hole smoothly, with a few strokes of his left foot. He swept the sand with a pine branch. He touched the sandbank, then stepped back, almost tripping over the old fire pit. He picked up one of the smaller stones and tossed it at the bank, just a soft lob. He touched his pocket. Nope, *never.*

"And now warming up for the Yankees, Maxwell Biedermann." His name was seventeen letters, too long to write on a baseball. Maybe he'd become so famous he could just write "Max" and everybody would know who he was, or they'd call him "Maximum" because he would become strong enough to pitch the ball at the maximum velocity—beyond which it would begin to warp and fall apart. Or it would be "Maximilian," because he was worth so much to the team. *Max a Million.*

He reached down and grabbed another stone, exactly the right size. He massaged it, as if the stone could be reshaped. He fired it into the soft embankment, where it disappeared. *Invisible pitch!*

"All right! Maximum really burned that one."

He could see the hole the stone had made. His eyes were excellent.

He dug for the stone. It had curved somehow and drilled six inches deeper into the embankment. He brushed wet sand from his arm, took the signed baseball out of his pocket, and lay stretched out on the soft ground for the next hour, rolling the ball across his chest, reading the names, mentally filling in the quarter inch where a bit of the ink had rubbed off. The names were mostly clear: Campanella, Hodges, Robinson, Reese, Snider, a few others he could not quite make out. He thought about the young Don Gerling, imagined him crying, gripping the doorframe as his mother tried to push him out of the house, into the real world. A future awaited him in the big city, a career with the Yankees, even better than the Dodgers, his name on a World Series game ball with eight other future Hall of Famers. But he wouldn't go; his mom stopped pushing, and when, after the war, he was too sick to do anything, she took care of him. They might have listened to distant ball games on his radio, in English and French, the signal sputtering into static.

Max thought about his own mother, how she would get into his belongings, how she could never tell the value of one thing over another—"They're all the same"—how she might look at this dirty ball and give it away. Or she might see John Gerling's name still clearly written (the others completely meaningless to her) and toss the ball in the garbage, swearing at the dead man for an unknown reason, a man who had actually played in the Majors. Max would find a proper hiding place.

This treasure safely in his pocket, he retreated toward the highway. He threw uprooted saplings over the path, pulled down live ones to block any future passage into this secret place.

East Branch, Lost River

Joshua was a hermit, in his eighties, a defrocked Methodist minister. He had last preached in Lost River, New York—a parish that must have eventually dissolved or merged with another, but such matters did not occupy Joshua's mind. Staying alive occupied most of that space: staying warm in winter, obtaining healthy food, dealing with the fact that he was squatting on state land. He never went to the doctor. No reason to. Occasionally he would think about the behavior that had led to his defrocking. The drinking, the adultery.

He'd been living in the wilderness for several decades, a long walk away from temptation.

His real name was Francis Asbury Biedermann, his "city name," a name given to him with high clerical expectations. He knew his church history.

Joshua wasn't a complete hermit. He paid rent for a post office box in Herkimer, which he visited once a month, attending to financial matters, and bought bulk food (powdered milk, Tang, noodles, etc.) and ballpoint pens. For his city errands, he owned a properly registered (if not inspected) 1965 Oldsmobile parked at the end of a logging road, nowhere near the trails that led to Lost River. The trails leading back to Lost River were worse than any labyrinth. He had his own private ten-mile route going in the opposite direction—southeast—mostly downhill from his shelter to his car, a route unmarked except by snowshoe tracks in winter. He never received letters from his former parishioners. They didn't know his location, and even if they tracked him down, they wouldn't recognize him: long white hair, long white beard. The stereotype of a hermit. He had been clean-cut and baby-faced the last time they saw him, his farewell sermon in the outdoor chapel behind the church. It was a lovely chapel, with split logs for pews, an altar covered with birch bark, a view of Hogback Mountain through a break in the white pines. The fire tower, which he had never visited, would sometimes reflect sunlight along its eastern side, a flash of brightness that flickered if he turned his head the right way.

During his time as a hermit, he'd become friends with the forest ranger assigned to the Loon Pond trailhead, where Joshua kept his car—year-round—and where two trails diverged, Joshua's private trail and the marked state trail leading to a tiny pond five miles to the northeast. He'd hiked there once and thought, *What's the fuss? And where's the loon?* The ranger had believed Joshua's story about his car being "grandfathered in." This was a January in the previous century, when Joshua had emerged at the parking area in snowshoes. The ranger had driven up to check the trailhead register.

"Nobody yet this winter," the young man had said.

"You don't have to include me. I never sign in. I'm permanent. Name is Joshua. You might have heard about me from the man you replaced."

"Actually, no."

"Good. And don't worry about the car," Joshua said. "Some days you might come by to check the register and find my vehicle covered by two feet of snow. Not to worry."

"I'll brush it off for you. Right now." Six inches of snow had fallen, which the ranger proceeded to clear with his right arm while Joshua watched, impatient about throwing his empty pack and snowshoes into the back of the car and heading down to the city. The gravel road to civilization had been recently plowed, including enough space to turn around at the trailhead. Joshua had a bank account in Herkimer, in which stock dividends were regularly deposited on his behalf, by relatives who assumed he was still alive, based on the occasional withdrawals. He never actually drove into town. He would park behind an abandoned strip mall and walk the last two miles. He was never stopped.

While in town, he would buy the Utica and New York City papers, for the crossword puzzles. The more difficult, the better, although the cultural references made him feel like a visitor from another planet. The news didn't interest him. When done with the newspapers, he would ball them up and stuff them in the

walls of his shelter or twist them into log shapes for
fire-starters.

The old lean-to was situated many miles from any
well-used trail, basically abandoned when a side trail of
the Northville-Placid was rerouted. Joshua's first September, he closed in the front of the shelter with wood
from the ruined outhouse and from another structure
disassembled long ago, the wood piled haphazardly,
crisscross, not yet rotten. He had brought with him a
hammer and a box of three-inch nails. The fireplace
was close enough to become an indoor fireplace when
the front was walled in. He constructed a chimney
with the most plentiful material at hand: rocks, which
he fit together without mortar. His fires for cooking
and heating were fueled by another material in plentiful supply: dead wood. Maple, yellow birch, beech.
Dead beech trees were especially plentiful.

Excellent water came from the East Branch of the
Lost River.

Normally, the journal of an Adirondack hermit would
be of interest to historians and museum curators.
Joshua had read several such books. No true confes-
sions in them, just everyday life in the wild, nam-
ing flora and fauna, mountains and lakes and ponds.
Joshua's journal was unpublishable. It named people.
He had stocked his shelter with paperback books on
many subjects, but no Bible, just a fancy commentary.
No *Book of Discipline*; he had burned his copy, page by

page. A battery-powered lantern hung from the ceiling, above the Adirondack chair he had built, imperfect but cushioned.

Decades ago, a Lost River inhabitant had stumbled into Joshua's shelter during a severe thunderstorm, a middle-aged man who wanted to tell his story, who felt safe telling it to a stranger. *Keep going*, Joshua would say. *Don't spare me the details. I won't judge you. I'm a sinner myself.* The man had led a terrible life, with the most ungrateful children. Nasty and violent. Joshua listened, saying nothing about his own children, who, he assumed, were grateful not to have him in their lives, mainly because of the drinking—every afternoon, even on Sundays, at a tiny bar in the middle of nowhere, run by a couple of ex-ballplayers who were around his age. Home Plate. Clever name.

He didn't believe that his children had tried very hard to track him down. Or that it was all his fault.

The strangest thing: one summer morning he got lost on his own trail, which he should have been able to walk blindfolded. It was as if someone had come through during the past month—in the time since Joshua believed he had last walked it—and superseded his trail with something similar, with red ribbons tied to the trees every hundred feet. It was as if by taking the superseding trail, following the red ribbon, Joshua might end up at an encampment much like his own, under the management of a similar hermit.

"I own this land," said the middle-aged man who had been tying the red ribbons to the trees.

"I think the state owns it." Joshua didn't want to argue. At the same time, he feared being expelled from the wilderness, like Adam and Eve out of the garden, who, as Joshua understood the Bible, had not been cast out for committing any sin, but merely for their knowledge of good and evil.

"They *think* they own it," the man said, smiling, cheerful, evidently lacking the temperament for arguing. "I have a deed, but not in my pocket. The damn thing weighs nearly ten pounds or I would carry it around with me, as proof."

"Okay, I believe you. I'm on my way to the trailhead. My car is there."

"They *do* own the trailhead," the man added. He gave Joshua a close look. "You really think you should be driving?"

"Weather seems fine," Joshua said. "No snow, no ice, maybe a bit of mud."

The man shook his head, caught his ball cap before it hit the ground. "I'm almost out of ribbon here and will be headed back to the parking area. Done for the day. I believe I saw your car down there. An Olds from the sixties?"

"Thereabouts."

"We'll walk together," the man said. "Here, take my cane." He handed Joshua a fancy walking stick with a leather strap tied through a hole on the thick end.

"You were going to say that I need it more than you do." But Joshua took it.

"Possibly true," the man said. "You look like you haven't eaten in a while."

Joshua never returned to his encampment. When they reached the parking area, the red-ribbon man waited while Joshua tried to get his car started. Not only was the battery dead, but the tires were flat, the windshield shattered.

"How long has it been?" the man asked.

"I thought, a month, but I might have missed one or two."

"Or a year, or two. Or ten."

"I tend to get busy and lose track of time." He brushed a thick layer of pine needles from the hood of his car.

"You're going to ride with me to the city," the man said in a loud voice, as if he thought Joshua was hard of hearing. "And then we'll figure things out."

"Herkimer?" Joshua said. "It's not really a city."

"Schenectady, which is. I have a B and B there."

"I've never heard of such a thing."

The man gave him a long look. "I'm the innkeeper. Please get in my car. We'll talk while I drive."

Joshua felt as if he was being taken to a kind of final reckoning, a process begun long ago. He may have been old—certainly looked old—but he wasn't ill. He wasn't feeble. He felt very strong, but he had a fairly good idea of the physical impression he'd made, from the way the man stared at him. Maybe he smelled bad. Or strange, like the balsam in his pillow. Now they were in Mayfield, then Galway, the western edge of Saratoga—close to the district office where the defrocking had taken place, a Methodist ritual that was nothing special, nothing visually interesting, merely a procedure in which one's misdeeds were detailed by the district superintendent, the consequences spelled out. The actual consequences for Joshua: a disappearance, a loss of family, a life in the woods, the loss of normal human contact. But that might be about to change, because of the innkeeper.

A house in Schenectady. He'd never been there. Long ago, he'd met people from Schenectady, fellow counselors at a church camp in the Adirondacks, all of them Methodist ministers or studying to be. He doubted he would ever run into them. Even if he shaved and cut his hair, they wouldn't know him. He might be able to glide his way toward the inevitable end—with the help of the innkeeper, or other people, strangers he would bless when he encountered them on the streets he would walk every day.

Counting Loons

1. Loons flying overhead should not be counted, to prevent duplicate observations of birds that were surveyed on another lake.

—Biodiversity Research Institute,
Saranac Lake, New York

July 20, 2014. The loon counters sat around the red picnic table in front of Olmsteads's store. Their identical T-shirts depicted a charcoal-gray loon family swimming left to right on a white background—two adults, two chicks. The loon counters also wore identical dark blue loon ball caps, except for Max Biedermann, who wore a Yankees cap. It was ten o'clock in the morning on "Loon Census Day" in the Adirondacks, the third Saturday in July. The eight participants were eager to share their results—all having, supposedly, done their observations during the earlier one-hour "window." Six of the eight had observed on various sections of Silver Lake, the other two on smaller lakes to the north.

Doug Sanders, a bald retired shop teacher, had counted loons on Little Silver Lake—forty acres, small enough for one person to cover. "I counted two adults and two chicks," he said, "but there was a problem."

"You actually *saw* all four of them, I hope," said Elise, the group leader, age sixty-plus, six feet tall, dyed-red frizzy hair, who stood imperiously at the end of the table through the entire meeting. "You can't count them if you only *hear* them."

"I got shot at."

Everybody laughed.

"No, really," Doug said. "It's not funny. There's a guy up there on Little Silver who thinks he owns the whole shoreline, most of which is actually state owned. I was observing from *state land*."

"Oh, that guy," Max said, twisting his Yankees cap slightly.

Most loon counters were older than Max. Some lived year-round in the Adirondacks, in winterized homes on the shores of Silver Lake. Unlike Max, they didn't have to work for a living. Max was a boat mechanic, with a dozen motors waiting in his shop.

"He's a psychopath," Doug said.

"He's harmless," Max said with a smile. "Monty LeBeau."

"He evidently missed," Elise said, jotting down Doug's observations. More laughter from the group around the table.

Doug stood up, took off his cap, and scratched his pale white head. He gazed warily toward the highway. "Two shots from a rifle, three seconds apart." He flinched, as if being fired at in that moment, as if practicing for a courtroom performance. "There might have been more loons to count on my lake, but I ran off and got in my car. Can you blame me?"

"Not at all," Elise said. "Your safety is more important than an accurate count, but just barely. Now sit down." Doug obeyed. Elise waited for the others to stop laughing, then said, "I observed on the north shore of the big island, and I will report that I saw a single loon flying overhead this morning, but he *did* land. I saw him clearly. He hit water twenty feet from my dock, at exactly eight-thirty. Kerplunk. Case closed."

"He?" one of the younger women said.

"Or she, though we don't need to be specific in our reporting. That's it for me, one adult loon. Last year I counted six. What's happening?"

"Geese," Max said. "There's, like, a hundred of them living on our lake now."

"You exaggerate," Elise said.

"Invasive. No fear of humans. We should post a geese crossing sign on Lakeshore Road. I waited in my car five minutes the other day while they crossed."

"A dozen on my lake," Doug said. "The psychopath feeds them."

"He's not a psychopath."

"No geese on *my* lake," Wesley said, an artist who lived a half hour north of where they sat. Young guy, around thirty, blond hair in a man-bun, oversize XXL loon shirt, rustic cross dangling from a wooden chain. A wooden chain being difficult to carve, Max figured this Wesley guy was showing off.

*1. Please sketch a map on the back of this form.
Please note if you conducted observations on the
entire lake or on a portion of the lake. Note where
the birds were observed, the direction in which they
swam or flew, and the location of the observer.*

The others knew little about Wesley's lake. "Here
it is," he said softly, unfolding the multicolored map he
had drawn. The loon counters leaned in for a closer
look. The lake was small, the birds were large, not just
X's showing where they'd been observed, but actual
Audubon-quality drawings, no larger than an inch, two
adult loons swimming south, as shown by a fancy direc-
tional arrow, followed by two chicks, even smaller than
the adults, the family creating a tiny wake. Wesley must
have used a magnifying glass to render the chicks.

The others marveled at the artist's skill, and even
more at the depiction of his camp—"like a luxury
hotel"—situated along the west shore of Mud Lake,
one of a dozen Mud Lakes in the Adirondacks, perhaps
the prettiest.

"I may exaggerate the splendor," Wesley said. "And
of course, the loons are not to scale. I observed them
from my dock. While seated."

"I have no dock," Doug said. "I stood on the shore
of Little Silver. My double-wide is not actually on the
lake, but I have access rights in my deed."

"That can be tricky," Wesley said. "Can you afford
a lawyer?"

"How much shoreline do *you* have?" Doug asked.

"The entire western shore of Mud Lake, a half mile total. There's one other camp on the opposite shore, a tiny enclave surrounded by state land. Summer residents. Russ and Linda Wolcott. They weren't around for the count. Today was actually my first time."

"You drew an *X* on dry land," Elise said, pointing with her pen. "Right here, on the peninsula that sticks out into your lake."

"It's not an *X*. It's a cross."

"Cemetery?"

"Chapel." He fingered his wooden cross. "My camp includes a chapel, a separate building close to the shore. Open-air."

"Lovely," two of the women said in unison.

"I'd like to worship there," one said, the woman with long dark hair.

Chapel, Max thought. *I've never been in a chapel. Or a church, for that matter.*

"Mud Lake," Doug said, sipping his coffee, setting it down carefully on the uneven tabletop. His hands shook. "Not the most attractive name."

"Keeps the riffraff out," Wesley said as he folded up his map.

"By the way," Max said, "how did you draw the map so quickly?"

"I drew the lake yesterday, added the loons this morning after I counted them."

"Amazing," Max said. "You could frame the map and sell it."

"I don't need the money."

An artist who doesn't need the money, Max thought. *An artist who owns a half mile of shoreline. Things are changing around here, or maybe they've always been this way and I'm just now finding out.*

1. An adult loon is fully feathered with black and white feathers, and is full size. A chick has either black or brown down and is less than two-thirds the adult size. An immature loon is fully feathered with light and dark gray feathers, and is two-thirds adult size or larger.

"We did the south shore of Big Silver," Cheryl Foxworth said, barely nodding at her husband James, who sat next to her, fingering his goatee. They were a foot apart and not looking at each other.

"Separate reports," James said, slowly.

"Separate boats. Kayaks. We'd be going around in circles if we shared the same boat."

"We can't have overlap," Elise said, articulating every syllable. "Our report needs to be accurate."

Max tipped his head back and closed his eyes. *This is ridiculous. What if the report isn't accurate? To tell the truth, it can't be accurate, since we're missing the remote lakes, the bodies of water large enough to have loons, if the pH level isn't too acidic. If there's fish, there's loons.* Elise should have known about the wilderness lakes and their uncounted loons. Right in the center of her twenty-thousand-acre private forest, north of Silver

Lake, were the Twin Lakes, both large enough to support a loon population. Elise had confessed to Max, "I've only seen my lakes from an airplane."

The previous Labor Day, Max had hiked deep into the wilderness and camped overnight on the shore of Rondeau Lake, one square mile—his secret lake, completely wild, no camps, no boats, with a natural sandy beach on the south shore where he built a campfire using driftwood. He sat on a log and watched the fire until it died. He awakened very early the next morning to a loud clatter of loons. He lay in his tent and listened until the clatter faded into a background of waves splashing on the beach. Those loons would never have been counted on any official loon Census Day—unless, during the one-hour "window," they had somehow landed on a lake near a highway, across from a great camp, a lake where rich people had nothing better to do than sit on their docks and count loons. Like this new guy, Wesley.

I don't need the money.

Max had drifted off, hadn't really missed anything. The others at the picnic table were still talking about separate boats and overlapping observations. Cheryl, his old babysitter from thirty years ago, was arguing with her husband, a city guy for sure. James. One time Max called him "Jim" and was reprimanded—like, "Not even my wife is allowed to call me Jim." Max imagined the shouting match that might have occurred when she mistakenly called her husband Jim. Perhaps they arm-wrestled over the issue. Cheryl looked strong enough to win. In his baggy T-shirt, James looked like he had no arm strength at all.

"Max!" Elise shouted.

"Yes, ma'am."

"I've asked you twice. How many at Narrow Bay, where you observed?"

"Zero. Didn't I already tell you?"

"Zero?"

"One flying above." He made a flying gesture with both hands. "Hope somebody saw him land. Him or her."

"Thank you," the woman with long dark hair said, with a beautiful smile. He'd never met her before. Black hair with a white streak. Martha, according to her badge. Evidently, she liked Max's pronouns, which seemed to matter in the counting of loons. Was she married? Hard to tell, with so many rings on her fingers.

1. *It is essential that the observations be conducted on the Census Day, from eight to nine a.m., and continue for the entire hour, to prevent duplicate observations.*

Martha turned to the rich young artist from Mud Lake and said, "Didn't I see a painting of yours the other day at the Town Museum? The local artists' exhibit that started this week?"

"Could be. I'm local. I'm Adirondack." He didn't even look at her, although she was obviously flirting.

"Wesley. That's you, right?"

"I guess I signed it," he said, with a quick glance toward Martha. "Most I don't sign, or the signature is so messy it may as well be anonymous."

"I know your mother," Elise said, pointing her pen at him. "Going way back. She brags about you."

Martha ignored her. "The title was *Sunset on Silver Lake*, with an empty canoe evidently drifting away. Beautiful. But you don't even live on Silver Lake."

"I was visiting," he said. "Friends on the Point. Did you like how I rendered the wake from the canoe? The colors?"

"Yes, perfect," Martha answered, almost singing. "A lost canoe. Which makes me wonder who lost it and how they felt about their loss."

"The painting's for sale," Wesley said. "You may have noticed."

"Okay, you two," Elise interrupted, "our business this morning is not art appreciation, as beautiful as those paintings might be. Or art sales, as *valuable* as they might be." She squinted at Martha's badge, to confirm the name. "What's your loon count for today, Martha?"

"I'm sure we have three. My husband Steve would confirm the number if he were here. He slept in. Three loons yesterday."

Okay, Max almost said out loud, *she's married*.

"But today?" Elise said. "This morning?"

"I guess zero. Now I feel like a complete loser." She leaned back and shook her marvelous black hair. She certainly did not look like a loser.

"No, not at all," Elise said. "This is relevant information, for when I send the report up to Saranac Lake."

Here we go again. Max felt like commenting on the paper pushers up in Saranac Lake and Ray Brook, the government and nonprofit workers whose greatest joy, evidently, was to collect the facts and then create wilderness policies disregarding those facts, but he merely closed his eyes. In his mind, he was back at Rondeau Lake, a three-hour hike from Jack Gerling's old place, the Home Plate, now in ruins. No chapel, never a chapel. What would a chapel have looked like? Did it need a roof? Did it need walls? Chairs? If not, then there could have been a chapel on Jack's property, or anywhere along the unmarked trail to Rondeau Lake. The beach could have been a chapel.

If he mentioned Jack, hardly anyone would know who he was talking about. Sometimes they would say, "What's with the Yankees ball cap?" and he would answer, "You wouldn't understand." He still had the Dodgers ball Jack had given him, with all the signatures. He had kept it in pristine condition and was thinking of donating it to the Town Museum. They could set up a "Baseball in the Adirondacks" exhibit. They could record Max talking about his time with Jack. Max could write a short essay to go with the display of the signed ball. He could write a decent paragraph.

Silver Lake people only knew Max as the boat mechanic. They might have remembered him pitching for the high school baseball team—Class D state champions, thanks to his one-hitter. Then he went to

Syracuse on a full-ride athletic scholarship, had to quit and return home before playing even one game. To take care of his mother. Some pitied him. They even told him that. It was time for him to get a wife. They even told him *that*.

A sharp "Hey!" interrupted his daydream. A male voice, loud and ragged, not from anyone around the table.

"Oh no," Doug said. "He tracked me down. Everybody duck!"

Rather than ducking, Max stood up and saw a familiar disheveled figure in the middle of the highway, pointing at them and shouting, "There's a loon," and "There's another loon," and "There's six more loons." Pointing a finger at each of the loon counters, not a gun.

One of the young women screamed. The box of T-shirts tipped over and fell on the ground. Elise screamed.

"I'm sure there's more of you," the man said. "You're ruining everything. And this loon here." He pointed at Doug. "Next time I see him on Little Silver. . . ." He paused.

"What?" Doug said in a high-pitch voice.

"You sound like a loon."

Traffic stopped. Horns honked. Max finally walked up to the man and said, "That's enough, Monty. You can walk back home now. We know who we are." It was the right thing to say for the occasion, but most of them around the table probably did not know who they were.

The Slicer

Regina repeated the words on the large brown sign along the edge of the road: ENTERING ADIRONDACK PARK. The sign marked the southwest border. She had walked northeast for two days before reaching it. The road eventually led to the place where she had worked as a teenager. The store been tiny back then, the entire left side interior taken up by a white deli case. Sandwiches for a dollar, with a free pickle. Homemade potato salad, and the cheap stuff in a can when the homemade ran out, a simple can opener kept on a hook under the counter. There were little rooms off to the side, for storage, and one room where the owners often retreated during the day, where they would drink until they collapsed on the floor. They were long dead, Regina figured, probably before the turn of the century.

Dead, like the man who might have been her father, an old baseball player who used to run a little hotel a few miles north of Silver Lake. He would be over a hundred if he was still alive. She had only known about him for a couple of years, having found several old letters in a box after her mother died, all signed with "Much love, Jack." Too late to ask whether her mother replied to any of the letters. She might have been very demanding. A poem needed to be written about it.

Back in the late sixties, Regina had worked at Silver Lake, the summer before she went off to college. She shared a cabin behind the store with another worker, Suzanne, whose last name Regina could not remember. Each had her own knotty-pine bedroom. They paid no rent, no utilities, and the refrigerator in the front room was stocked with free food, including sandwiches from the deli, unclaimed, a day old, sometimes two days old. A certain customer, ancient even then, possibly born in the nineteenth century, would stop by the deli counter every morning, right when the store was opening, and put in his sandwich order—"The usual, and don't you dare change a thing." He would return an hour later with his mixed-breed dog and eat the sandwich while seated on the front porch next to the newspapers, which he read without paying for them. The workers would watch from the window and laugh, as the pieces of meat fell from his mouth, only to be quickly consumed by the dog, often before the meat hit the floor. Suzanne had a nickname for the old man: "Quarter Pounder."

Even Suzanne might be dead by now.

Regina kept up a good pace. By her rough calculation, she was now at least ten miles inside the Adirondack Park.

The highway had a wide shoulder, with the stylized white figure of a bicyclist painted on the dark pavement every hundred yards. Regina had seen no three-dimensional bicyclists. Since morning, she had sucked on two lemon cough drops. She had scooped water out of a pothole and rinsed her mouth with it, tried not to swallow, although any dead insects or plant life would have been nutritious, a benefit. In her mind, she kept a list of benefits, a list she would frequently review.

A blue convertible passed by slowly, filled with teenage boys. They whistled and yelled, "Hey, beautiful!" She ignored them. She had once been beautiful, by any measure—one of five girls on her high school's prom court, which was impressive in a high school with a graduating class of four hundred. Long ago she had torn the prom-photo page from the yearbook, and still carried it with her in her backpack. The photo was fuzzy, and filthy. The photo wasn't something she would whip out to prove a point about who she was. She knew who she was: a seventy-year-old woman with a long white braid, probably a few leaves and pine needles stuck to it. She weighed two hundred pounds, perhaps more. She hadn't weighed herself in a decade.

She had slept well the night before—in the balsam woods on the fringe of a public campground just outside the Blue Line. She had bushwhacked into the place, avoiding the entrance gate where she might have been denied entry. Under the cover of darkness she had snuck into the campsite latrine, which had flush toilets and nice sinks, a motion-activated light. Showers. Her bed in the woods was a pile of fluffed-up dead leaves and balsam needles. For a pillow, her backpack. Her bivouac lay a hundred feet from a family in a tent trailer. The children in that family had misbehaved. The father, in what might have been an Italian accent, yelled at one of them: "No desserta for a weeka!"

D-Zerta. An awful variation on Jell-O that Regina's mother would force on her and her little brother. Lemon flavor, orange flavor, bad texture, no natural ingredients. *You're better off eating bugs, worms, grubs! Be grateful!*

A car slowed as it passed, then came to a complete stop, a fancy white SUV, with an ADK bumper sticker. Animal rights stickers, abortion rights, SUNY Cortland, next to a fierce red dragon. The driver got out, a woman of no particular age wearing a plaid flannel shirt, khaki pants, and tan work boots. She wore a paper badge, as if she were attending a convention. The badge read, HELLO, I'M CHERYL. The woman stood defiantly, as if to confront Regina, as if there were a warrant out for her arrest on an ancient vagrancy charge. This Cheryl could have been a plainclothes cop in an unmarked car. They had finally tracked Regina down. Unpaid bills, unpaid rent.

"Ma'am," the woman said, like a cop.

"I'm minding my own business," Regina said.

"I can give you a ride."

Ridiculous, unwanted. A ride to hell? Rides seldom turned out to her benefit, usually in some form of custody. "I'm fine."

"You look like you could use a good meal."

"That's your opinion." Regina smiled. Her teeth probably looked like jack-o'-lantern teeth. "I actually need to lose weight. I need the exercise."

"I beg to differ."

What a strange thing to say! Beg to differ? Where did that come from? From a book? The Bible? Regina laughed. "I'm hiking this morning, so it would be cheating to accept a ride from anyone. Nice of you to offer."

The woman shook her head, got back in her car, and rolled down the window and spoke to Regina as she walked by. "Listen," she said. "I will check on you again in a couple hours."

"Don't bother."

"Oh, it's no bother. I have to drive back to Utica anyway. My husband and I have a camp on Silver Lake that I check for mice once a week, which takes less than an hour, and then I drive back to the city until next Saturday. Sometimes I pick the wild raspberries. I could bring you a cup of raspberries. In a Ziploc bag."

"Utica?" Regina stopped walking.

"Yes," the woman said. "Actually, New Hartford."

"Silver Lake?"

"Yes, eight miles from here."

"Good to know," Regina said.

"In addition to the bag of raspberries, I could order and pay for a sandwich at the store and it would be ready for you when you get there." Way too cheerful.

"I'm not headed to the store," Regina lied.

"Their sandwiches are terrific. Do you have any preferences? Is meat okay? They do have vegan options."

Regina said nothing. The interrogation was over. She kept moving east, away from this demanding woman. She turned her head toward the forest, thinking she might randomly enter it. She'd done that before, at other Adirondack locations, having grown tired of highway walking, or curious about what lay within.

"Ma'am? Ma'am!"

Regina gave her a dismissive, over-the-shoulder wave. The woman triple-honked at her when she drove away, as if to insult her, like the teenage boys. But the encounter had provided two benefits:

> 1. The comment about Regina's body, that she needed a meal, which might mean she had lost weight. That was good.
> 2. The possibility of a sandwich waiting for her at the Silver Lake store, where she had worked decades ago.

Both benefits had a downside, however. That she looked like she needed a good meal may have implied that she looked terrible, gaunt, wrinkled, as if she had aged badly. She fingered her upper lip. Whiskers? Possibly.

A fancy sandwich waiting for her at Silver Lake had complications. Like, how would she identify herself? The only ID she had on her was a handwritten poem she had signed and dated. And if there was no sandwich waiting, then she would seem crazy for having asked about it, like, *There was this woman along the highway who stopped her car beside me and said she would buy me a sandwich*? Who would believe such a claim? And what if the sandwich existed, but had pickle relish mixed in with it? Or horse radish. It would be unpalatable. And she hated raspberries!

Robert was a boy she liked when she was a teenager, a boy who spent his summers at the lake. He stayed with his rich grandfather on the north shore of Silver Lake. He would sit on the front porch of Olmsteads's and play his guitar while waiting for his sandwich. He always requested bologna and cheese on wheat bread, lots of mayo, no lettuce, and expected that Regina would make it for him. "Put it on my grandpa's bill."

One afternoon she was on break when the meat for Robert's sandwich was being sliced, and he was pointing at the slicer because the store clerk had been slicing the meat too thick. He got too close—perhaps due to poor depth perception—and the tip of his left index finger was cut off. A small piece, mostly skin, no bone. He didn't scream, didn't cry, but he gave up playing the guitar (the left index finger being essential to forming most chords, he said) and he would look at Regina as if it had been her fault for not being there (in which case Robert would not have needed to point and would not have lost the tip of his index finger). He had been a poet, too, and he gave that up, which made no sense. When she would ask him if he had another poem for her, he acted like she was crazy. Years later, she wrote several poems about Robert, various hikes they might have taken in the Adirondacks. She wanted to share those poems with him. Maybe he still visited his grandfather on Silver Lake. Would she even recognize him? No way would he recognize *her*.

After the finger incident, rules were posted in the store, requiring customers to stand at least three feet from the slicer while it was being operated.

Her cabin mate often didn't spend the night in the cabin, and when, out of concern for Suzanne's safety, Regina mentioned this to the owner, she had told Regina to mind her own business. It turned out Suzanne was dating the owners' brother, Abraham, age forty-something. By the end of the summer, the two of them had run away to parts unknown.

A collapsed roadhouse came into view on the other side of the highway. A tree had grown out of the middle of the building, and then died. The unlit neon sign in front read DEMARESTS, as if there were more than one person by that name besides the man who ran the place, and Regina began to think she had spent time in that ruined building, but the probable truth was that she had only dreamed of being inside, dancing alone in front of a crowd, under a bright light, a dream based on fears about what might have happened to Suzanne. Dancing on a table, in public. Not as bad as the dream her brother had posted in his blog two years ago, so detailed it had to have been true—how he had entered what he thought was a mall, somewhere upstate, which turned out to be the intake location for a prison, with two dozen tough guys sitting on benches in front of an array of tiny gray lockers. Inside one locker, he had found a pair of dark blue flip-flops, which he had put on, since he had arrived barefoot. Regina had thought, *Why is he sharing this with the world? Does he think I might still have a computer, and regularly read his blogs?* She was using the computer in the Utica Public Library. At the end of the supposed dream, her brother had walked free, out of the opposite end of the mall and onto the Northville-Placid Trail. Whatever crime he'd committed, he never did time for it. But flip-flops? On a long hike? Regina wore Limmer boots—bought twenty years ago, when she had money.

A half hour east of the old roadhouse, a brown sign marked an official turnoff: trailhead parking. Mt. Osborne. *Okay*, she thought, *I'll be a hiker for a minute. I told the bossy woman I was hiking, so I'll make it less of a lie. Of course, I'd still be guilty of deception, but that's nor-mal.* A white pickup truck was parked diagonally at the trailhead, no one inside. Regina walked slowly through knee-high grass toward a small dark wooden struc-ture—a kiosk—where, as she understood the rules (if the rules hadn't changed since the previous century), hikers registered their existence and intentions. Very few had registered since the previous year, only one full page. After all, there was no writing implement, just a wad of pink gum, pink sunglasses, and a matching pink comb. Regina took a freebie ballpoint pen from her shirt pocket and signed in. Purple. In the DESTI-NATION box, she drew a question mark. Everybody else had written "tower," though she hadn't noticed any mountain, so it might have been quite a long hike to reach any tower, and it might have been the kind of tower where all the steps had been ripped out. On the kiosk shelf Regina found an Orangina bottle, half full. She drank it, though the label said it contained only 10 percent fruit juice. She needed the sugar.

One entry in the logbook read, "Try the Blue Mountain! Cheese and meat and cheese and meat and cheese, a foot tall!" The entry was from two summers ago. The sandwich might have shrunk since then. Probably not as many layers.

She kept her purple pen. She needed it to write a poem.

Suzanne had written a letter to Regina's little brother, then only twelve years old. The envelope was post-marked in California, and the letter was full of short poems and dopey philosophy and a hint that Suzanne was breaking the law. Still with Abraham, evidently. The letter was another object that Regina carried in her backpack. It weighed almost nothing—physically. Emotionally, quite a bit. The benefit was that she had taken it away from her brother before he could read it. Thinking about the *naughty letter* sitting at the bottom of her backpack was a mix of good and bad. Good, that she had it; bad, that it existed.

She hardly recognized the store—brown, instead of salmon pink. The front porch was much larger, but had no newspaper rack. In the old days, there had been two racks for the newspapers from Albany, Saratoga, Utica, Syracuse, New York City, and a stack of reserved papers inside next to the cash register.

There were three bright red picnic tables out front. All were occupied, a dozen people wearing loon T-shirts and identical dark blue caps, talking about different parts of the lake. *That was my loon, etc.* Cars towing motorboats were lined up at the gas pumps—a new brand of gas. Regina had expected people to stare at her, but they were indifferent, preoccupied with their silly lives, their impossible children demanding double-dipped cones with a cherry on top, screaming, "Or else!" Regina stepped onto the porch. The bulletin board listed a wide variety of lost items: a one-eyed cat, a canoe paddle, a wallet, a life preserver, a fifty-dollar bill. A business card advertised stump removal. Why couldn't they just let the stump stay where it was?

Someone named Robert had posted an index card: "Writing group tonight. Don't forget." *Her* Robert? No details about when or where, as if this information were a closely held secret known only by the Silver Lake in crowd.

Inside, a young man in a red shirt operated the meat slicer. A store logo was printed in white on the shirt. Was he even old enough? Wasn't there a law that you had to be at least eighteen? Regina stepped close to the slicer. She asked the young man, "Are you just going to toss those scraps? That's good roast beef!"

"It's the rough end. People don't want it."

Regina held her hand under the moving blade, to catch the pieces. "I want it."

She expected him to criticize her for being so bold, but he kept slicing and saying, "No problem," which young people said all the time, even when multiple problems existed beyond their imagination.

"I can't pay you anything," she said, grabbing a nearby Ziploc bag and stuffing the scraps inside, at first unaware of the piece of meat hanging from the corner of her mouth, then catching it with her tongue. "Tastes good," she said.

"My boss might be watching upstairs."

"Really?"

"There's cameras all over," the boy said. "She might not like what she sees, but she's always telling us to be nice to the customers."

"I used to work here."

"In that case, would you like some cheese to go with the meat?"

"You weren't even born then. Your *parents* probably weren't even born then." She grabbed another Ziploc bag and filled it with irregular pieces from the end of a cheddar loaf, while the young man nodded approvingly.

"I hope they pay you a lot of money," Regina said.

It might have been the same slicer from fifty years ago, from the time of the finger slicing and the end of the guitar playing and poetry writing. Probably a new blade. Blades might have to be replaced every couple of years. Regina was unfamiliar with store technicalities. The price per pound—irrelevant, because the scraps were free. She didn't even have a wallet, just a bunch of loose change jingling inside her pack. On the wall behind the deli case, a huge illuminated sign described the variety of sandwiches one might order—all costing twelve dollars, with a small bag of chips included. The Blue Mountain, The Silver Lake Islands, The Fire Tower, The Narrow Bay, The Olde Canoe, and The Build-Your-Own. She tried to imagine the layers that would justify twelve dollars. It would be the kind of sandwich you'd have to break down thoroughly in order to eat it, layer by layer, share it with a hungry dog, or a vagrant.

Regina never asked about the sandwich that had been vaguely promised earlier in the day, nor the bag of raspberries she would have smiled at but eventually tossed into the woods, somewhere along the remainder of her trek into the middle of the Adirondacks. It had become her habit, over the past several years, to walk away from things. Like her brother, she would continue to walk away from whatever the so-called regular people wanted to give her, of which the benefits seldom balanced out the burdens. She unfolded the poem from her pants pocket, kissed it lightly, and then tacked it to the bulletin board next to Robert's writing group reminder:

Every mountain has an inside,
A voice that calls out
From between rocks and trees,
Heard above a splashing stream,
A distant call for help.

The Guard

1.

*Three in a red canoe, crossing Mud Lake toward
my place, great diagonals, paintable.*

The visitors were shaped like generic canoeists at
first—identically angled heads and arms, as abstract as
a highway sign directing tourists to a canoe route. Then
I made out the faces of my across-the-lake neighbors,
Russ and Linda Wolcott. Who else could they be? I
saw their lips moving, the words inaudible, obscured
by the splash of paddles. They could have been talking
about me or about my place, how they liked or hated it.
Their matching single braids swung gently in unison.
The third person, the one in the middle, braidless, was
a stranger, not moving, two-dimensional.

From my second-floor studio, high above the flat
water, I saw an undeviating line of *V*'s pointing toward
my shore as the canoe pulled closer. I pictured the line
completing itself at my dock, and my own body in a
sequence of stop-motion shots, meeting the visitors at
the waterfront, performing polite gestures, getting rid

of them efficiently. I pictured myself the way a security camera would, as a discontinuity of gray silhouettes. I would be wearing my floppy L.L.Bean hat, in which the bulk of my hair was hidden.

I set my paintbrush in a tall glass of mineral spirits and cursed all the way to the boathouse. Some other time I might have welcomed my visitors with genuine good humor, but they had disturbed the flow of my painting, mid-stroke. I had been fixing a thin cusp of late afternoon sunlight on the high shoulder of an imaginary snow-capped mountain, and in my head, the source of light had already begun to shift and dim. I might lose it if distracted even for thirty seconds. The old red-and-yellow flag would have come in handy, the one my parents would hang from the boathouse when I was a boy. It supposedly meant, *We're resting, please come back later,* and in those days I would set out in my rowboat, oblivious to the truth, adrift on this same lake until the flag came down.

As I approached the visitors, I wiped my hands with a ragged towel, which I then tossed against the side of the boathouse. So often had I tossed a wet-paint towel against the boathouse that the wall began to look like a Jackson Pollock painting, with its random colorful drips. The other buildings on my property were dark and weathered, asking to be painted.

Russ and Linda pulled themselves out of the canoe, but the person in the middle remained seated, adjusting the straps on his bright yellow life jacket. Tightening or loosening, undecided. He held a lit cigarette and tapped his ashes into the lake. I could have said, *If the lake were larger, I wouldn't mind so much.*

"We won't visit more than a few minutes," Linda said. "We know how busy you are." Her usual sarcasm.

"Who's the passenger?"

They told me his name. He wanted to see my camp. I leaned over and held out my right hand. He grabbed it hard, used my strength to exit the boat. There were welts on my skin after he let go, the imprint of bone or metal.

"Thanks," he said. His hair appeared to be dyed black—a shiny, purplish black. He took one last drag and tossed his cigarette into the lake. "You live here?"

"Yes." The cigarette spun on the surface, then sank, which seemed odd. "Me and the fish, too," I added.

"Ungrammatical," the stranger said.

"Show Bruce around the estate," Russ said, gesturing with his canoe paddle. "Give him the grand tour." Russ and Linda jumped back into the canoe and pushed off abruptly, knocking against the old tires that protected the side of the dock. "We're doing the entire shoreline," Russ shouted. "Back in an hour, if the wind cooperates. You don't mind, do you?" I'm sure they had something else in mind. Plans that didn't involve their visitor.

"Go ahead." But I wasn't about to give any grand tour.

They pushed off, braids moving in slow unison. They really looked like twins. If two people eat the same food, think the same thoughts, and paddle the same canoe long enough, they become twins. Far from envying such a high degree of compatibility, the absorption of one person into another, I feared it greatly.

The stranger—Bruce—touched the wall of the boathouse, scratched the rough, dark brown surface. "This is very old," he said, putting his mouth to the wood, lips slightly puckered. "It tastes good. Like spice. Hundreds of years old."

"Not quite. My place was built in the thirties."

"Do you know who built it?"

"My grandparents," I said softly.

"We've been talking about it. Russ and Linda gave me the details. They said robber barons built it."

I laughed. "My grandparents weren't robber barons. That was an earlier generation."

"Don't be so defensive. I have nothing against rich people. I owe my livelihood to the generosity of rich people."

"My grandparents weren't rich."

"Oh, we've been talking," he said, "making up what was plausible when we didn't have the facts. Often you get at the truth that way."

"My grandparents were missionaries. Methodists. They weren't rich."

"Quakers."

"No, Methodists. Which is why my name is Wesley."

He wasn't listening, didn't get the connection between the religion and the name. Most people didn't.

"That they would be Quakers intrigues me," he said. "So much silence. Scary. Thinking about their sins." He pointed toward the lake, but the red canoe had disappeared. "Over there, Wes, on the other side, where the common people live, the three of us *common folk* sit and stare and speculate. You in your enormous mansion. One would think we could find better things to do with our time."

"It's Wesley. Is your time running out?"

"Almost," he said. "I've been up from the city since Tuesday, heading back tomorrow. We talked about coming over. Russ and Linda don't have a phone, of course, or we would have called ahead."

I told him about the pay phone at the Silver Lake store, left out the fact that it was often not working.

"The store wasn't on our route. At least a mile the other direction, right?"

"Actually, you have to drive there, twenty miles away."

"I get your drift," he said.

But he didn't. We were still outside. Bruce lit a fresh cigarette and looked over his shoulder toward the lake. He had an extremely thin neck, a "pencil neck," suitable for turning a watchful head, but otherwise impractical. "We planned to cruise by, slowly," he said. "Keep our distance from the shoreline. But then you walked out on this massive dock, so we decided to be sociable. Just an impulse!"

"Uh-huh." I wasn't on my dock when they decided. How many lies would I hear in the next hour?

"They told me you never had company." He tapped his ashes into the water.

"Not true." Why would they have told him anything about me? "Russ and Linda canoe over here maybe once a month for lunch."

"Overnight company, I meant."

"I take care of the camp for my parents." As if I needed a reason not to have overnight company. As if I were sixteen, with rules. But my parents had never placed restrictions on my use of the camp. In fact, they were about to deed it over to me. They hated the place—not the buildings, but the remote location, too far from their doctors. The lack of direct sunlight. They complained about feeling a chill even in summer. My mother called once a week to check on me. *At least* once a week.

"Does the isolation make you happy?" The visitor dropped his cigarette, stepped on it, then picked up a canoe paddle and read the label, then set it down again. He still had his life jacket on.

"It's okay," I said.

"Just okay?"

I led him up the steps and into the front room of the main lodge. Or, more accurately—I walked that way and he followed, carrying the towel I had wiped my hands on. He sniffed it. "Is this paint?" he asked. "Smells like paint."

"No, it's blood." I grabbed the towel, threw it toward the kitchen.

"Blood?"

"No, it's ketchup."

"You had a cookout?" He asked for a glass of water and sat on a wooden chair, still in his life jacket, and covered his face, then inspected his hands, his long dirty fingernails. What image were those nails supposed to convey? Depression? Laziness? If he was a painter, such nails might accidentally scrape the paint from his canvas, or, if he worked in pastels, the nails would make it hard to grip the chalk after he'd used up half its length. He might have been a conceptual artist who merely described his art and left it to others to execute it. The long nails might have been part of the concept—that he had deliberately hobbled himself and his art had suffered. Or he might not have been an artist.

He took a sip of tap water, frowned, then gazed up at the ceiling, the rough-cut timber that crisscrossed every which way; the rather bad-taste antlers chandelier too high up for me to do anything about, including the burned-out bulbs and huge cobwebs. "You have a second floor," he said. He pointed toward the balcony, the open loft, beyond which were half a dozen rooms he would never see.

"What do you do besides this?" Bruce asked as he set his glass on a birch twig table. He finally removed his life jacket, hung it from my antler coatrack. His red flannel shirt, partly unbuttoned, covered a black tanktop or T-shirt.

"Besides taking care of the camp?"

"When summer's over," he said, reclaiming his chair, sprawling in it.

"Oh, I stay here. I'm the year-round caretaker."

"Caretaker. What a sweet word!"

"Much more to take care of in winter. Summer is a vacation, compared to winter."

"Repair work?"

"Staying alive," I said. "A full-time job."

"I know."

I turned to look at him. One eye was covered by the flop of black hair. The other didn't seem to have an eyebrow. I cleared my dry throat. "They said you work in the city?"

"Four days on, four days off, like an airline pilot," he said. "Yeah, I work. I'm a guard at an art museum."

"Until you find something better."

"Like, a job as a caretaker. Wouldn't the two jobs be similar?"

Clearly he had things to say about being a guard, but I was anxious to get back to my painted mountain upstairs before the good light faded, before the shapes collapsed, the ones I held in my head, briefly. I should have told him. Instead, like a fool, I asked about his job.

He groaned and said, "For you, I'll break rule number one." He touched his hair, revealed the hidden eye, also eyebrow-less. "The rule is not to talk about my job while I'm out of the city. I told my friends to tape my mouth shut if I broke the rule."

"I'm sorry."

"No, it's just that I spend most of my time on the job thinking about what I'll do when I get off. Doesn't make sense to do the reverse, does it?"

"No."

"So when I'm working, I plan my escape. I visualize how I'll dash to the employees' lounge and change out of my guard uniform, grab my duffel and hurry to the train station. Ten blocks, ten minutes." He stood up and acted the way he evidently would in the city, jerking like a puppet, with hand signals, jogging in place, quick head movements. Ugly. I preferred not to have city life reenacted in my camp. There were Tiffany lamps that might be knocked over, my mother's Rookwood pottery, her Finnish crystal, my stacks of valuable art books. I figured Bruce was a frustrated actor who had thrived in college but washed out in the real world. "Now I'm at Zabar's," he said, hands still flailing. "I pick up a cinnamon pastry and eat it, feeling the sharp edges, the texture, the sweetness I crave—another ten minutes, while I wait in line." He went on to say he felt "cheated" by the dirty train windows on the trip up the Hudson and wondered if I had ever taken the train to New York. He sat down and stretched his legs.

I told him I hadn't been to New York City for many years.

"By choice?"

"It just never happened."

"That's no way to advance your career," he said. "The train ride is kind of romantic. I picture myself stepping off at Amsterdam, walking to a little car I would keep parked there all summer. The sun is always shining."

"Utica would be closer."

"I didn't know that," he said.

"And then you drive to the lake and visit with Russ and Linda. Or they pick you up."

"We were best friends at St. Lawrence. They're still nice to me." He yawned. "Which is amazing."

Why would it be amazing? Russ and Linda were nice to me, which I didn't consider in the least bit amazing. I considered it somewhat calculating. This man may have always talked that way, fishing for compliments, like my mother, who lately had been wondering aloud why my father still loved her, what he still found attractive about her in her old age. They were both in their early sixties. My mother kept asking, and my father said nothing, and I was supposed to fill the silence with a different topic.

Bruce leaned forward and hugged himself. "But while I'm standing there in the museum, it's like, I'm not even *there* anymore. I'm here. I mean across the lake, with Russ and Linda. And they're taking care of me, feeding me, comforting me. You know their place?"

"Very cozy."

"One way to describe it, compared to this mansion! How many rooms do you have?"

"Twelve. Not including the outbuildings."

"And how many of *those* do you have?" he asked.

"Five or six. Actually eight, if you include outhouses."

"Wow."

"Eight or nine. I forgot to include the chapel."

"I like that," he said. "Not knowing the exact number. Five or six or seven or ten. I wish I didn't know the exact number of my rooms in the city."

I took the cue. "How many?"

"One. Ha! And it's a closet. I'm lucky to have two windows. I've already counted a dozen here from where I'm sitting."

There were at least a dozen more that he could not see, *and would not see.*

"My rent is three thousand a month," he said. "More than half my take-home pay." He hugged himself tightly, as if he felt a chill. It was eighty degrees inside my camp, and I was sweating. I would have removed my hat, but I didn't want him to see my hair and talk nonsense about it. "So," he continued, "I stand there in my uniform and imagine what I'll do once I get up to the lake."

"I thought this was your first time in the Adirondacks."

"The conversations. The wonderful meals. The swimming. The hikes. I imagine new trails into the wilderness, waterfalls, mountains." He shaped them with his long fingers, although he shaped them all the same. "Most of the things I imagine probably don't exist. But I see them clearly. New people."

"You see the future?"

"No, the future never turns out the way I see it. But my imagination takes me away from that awful museum. I told you how bad it is. I stand in a windowless room eight hours a day with a bunch of huge black-and-white abstract paintings. New York School, late fifties?"

I nodded.

"Complete garbage," he said. He hated them. He hated the artists.

"You could fire bullets into those paintings."

"Museum guards don't carry guns." He frisked himself.

"Whack them with your billy club."

"Not even that."

"Then what kind of guard are you? How safe are those paintings from thieves and vandals?"

"Not very. All I do is tell people not to touch them—little kids who get too close, swinging their arms, pushing each other. If people ask about the paintings, I tell them what I know, the life of the artist, the scandal. Always a scandal."

He looked at me. I said nothing. He might have thought I would share something, or he already knew about it, from talking with Russ and Linda. I looked out the triple window, twelve feet high, with a great view of the lake and the rocky cliff on the opposite shore. The opposite shore was trail-less, inaccessible.

"Guards have to be careful," Bruce said. "There are plainclothes museum officials all over the place posing as real people. Guards aren't authorized to talk about paintings. We could get fired."

"I don't care for modern art," I said. "Most of it."

He smiled. I had said the right thing. A mistake—it encouraged him.

"They were supposed to rotate me to a different room. *Months* ago. I'd really like to guard the sculptures for a while—outside, in the sculpture garden. If I worked in the garden, I could smoke."

I doubted that. Finally, I asked if he was an artist.

"Depends on what you mean by 'artist.' I would hesitate to call myself anything, because I rely on other people to tell me what I am. I'm nobody unless you call me somebody."

"Me?"

He waited; I said nothing. "Worth a try," he continued. "I make art sometimes. Or I try to. Then I ask people what they think, hoping for honesty. If I had a sketchpad and a box of pastels right now I'd be pretty happy. It doesn't take much to make me happy. But I blame myself for forgetting to bring my art stuff this week. Big mistake." He tilted his head, awaiting my answer. He expected me to go get a sketchpad and pastels for him. "It really doesn't take much," he said.

"The view is great," I said. "I've never grown tired of it." I didn't mention the art I had created upstairs, inspired by the views I enjoyed every day, every month of the year. There were a dozen unfinished paintings in my studio, landscapes. Bruce might want to *guard* them. I figured my friends had matched the two of us that way, artist and art guard, and this Bruce already knew about my art—in general. Upstairs, not just landscapes, but paintings of human subjects. Like the life-size portrait of "Martha." A nude. And hidden in a locked drawer, a photo she took of me putting the final touches on that painting.

"I'd be happy," Bruce said, "simply sketching the bizarre angles on your boathouse, the approach of the red canoe, the waves crisscrossing. I'm pretty good with pastels, charcoal. I'm known for my colors, the way I mix and still keep them separate. If I had money, I'd buy a decent camera."

"You should see this lake in the off-season." I went to the side window with a direct view of the dock and waved at Russ and Linda, who were tying up.

Linda called out, "Did we come back too soon?" What did she think we were doing?

"No problem!" I shouted back. "We're ready."

Bruce put on his life jacket. "We are?"

I mumbled about having things to do before sunset.

"You were going to tell me something. The off-season?"

"Much more beautiful then. Much more peaceful."

"Is that an invitation?" Bruce asked.

"What do you mean?"

"What you said sounded like an invitation to me. A minute ago you said I should see the lake in the off-season."

I had never intended my remark to be taken literally. "Actually," I said, "I would strongly advise against driving up here. Not much happens all winter. No boating, no swimming, hard to get the car started.

Nobody around. Forty below zero. Ten feet of snow. Terrible driving."

"Which doesn't matter. Although you're lying."

"Don't risk your life." I had often told city friends they should visit me in the winter, and they said they longed for it, but rarely made the trip. They would write and tell me how screwed-up their lives had become, how inaccessible my place was in winter. "Wish we were there." And in a way, I wished the same, on dark afternoons when my art failed me and I needed good company. The point of having a place like this should have been to make other people happy. Not to make *me* happy, as I had long ago adjusted to its beauty and comfort, to the point where I would suddenly feel a sense of great dread and unhappiness wash over me from an invisible stream, a deep chill, a premature freeze in the blood.

We now stood on the dock.

"Everything I do, I risk my life," Bruce said, putting on his life preserver. "Otherwise, I have no life."

I felt a bit of deep chill, said nothing.

"See ya!" he said, stepping into the red canoe. "Don't be a stranger! Be happy!" He sat facing the rear of the canoe, dipping one hand in the water. Facing me. Russ and Linda paddled slowly, as if Bruce had told them not to hurry. He took in the beauty of my camp, saving it for himself, assuming ownership of it. I could see his lips moving. He put a cigarette in his mouth. It flicked up and down to the rhythm of his speech. I hoped never to see this person again.

The wake of the canoe played out in soft folds, the water so calm it reminded me of a vanilla pudding about to solidify and form a skin. I kept my eyes on the wake, ignored the canoe and its passengers. Bruce was a talker. He must have been talking about me. I loved the pattern the waves made when they crossed. Later, in August, I worked it into a good painting in which the canoe has evidently disappeared behind a point of land. You see only the wake, the clouds, the opposite shore, and the end of the dock from which the canoe has departed, the weathered boards, several wet footprints about to evaporate. *That* specific.

2.

"Maybe you shouldn't keep the driveway plowed," he said, his voice several sizes too large and entirely unwelcome. Uninvited. Early January, I had adjusted to silence. The slightest tick of a branch against the roof could be deafening.

He took off his boots and set them next to the fireplace, where I had a rather nice maple fire going, logs stacked nearby, not too close. A crackling fire, the sweet smell of maple wood burning. My visitor pulled off his ski cap, tossed it against the wall. His hair—light brown and three inches long—stood up funny from the static electricity. His neck was not so pencil-like, as if he'd worked on it since I last saw him.

"Why not?" I asked. "Why not plow it?"

"Discourage the riffraff." He laughed. "Not that I'm riffraff, but I parked my car along the highway and walked down, in case your parking lot was full. Very pretty. It's prettier now than in the summer."

"I have to get in and out. I pay a woman to plow it. I have to eat, you know."

"Couldn't you just stock up on everything, use powdered milk, canned meats and vegetables, and then let it snow and snow and never go out for weeks, months?"

"I could."

"I think you would. You remind me of a hermit."

I closed my eyes.

"So—why *don't* you leave it unplowed?" Voice too loud again. And who else in the entire Adirondack Park needed to hear this guy?

I made up something about my parents wanting the place to look occupied, how the locals who ride around on snowmobiles might get ideas from an unplowed driveway.

"What's to steal?" my visitor asked.

"Break a few windows, knock down a couple utility poles. Out of spite. Come in here and steal my lamps."

"Then at least you'd have something to do," he said, as if my life needed this change—vandals, chaos, provocation.

"I have plenty to do," I said.

"What? Tell me! Take off your hat."

He was referring to my black wool ski cap, silk-lined, very comfortable. I kept it on. I pushed the fire screen to one side and dropped a fresh maple log on the coals. The bark flared up. I knew the log would burn well. It had seasoned two decades in the wood-shed without rotting. My father had chopped down that tree, by hand, with an axe. Many times I had opened the woodshed door and looked at that specific log and had put off burning it, a deferred pleasure. Deferred pleasures were the extent of my happiness at Mud Lake. The happiness lasted as long as the plea-sure was deferred.

"So, you found your way without much trouble," I said.

"Easy trip. Linda drew a beautiful map. Is it okay for me to sit down?"

"Yeah. Okay. Anyplace is fine." I remained stand-ing. *Linda had drawn a map.* A work of art, no doubt, perhaps an homage to those medieval maps showing dragons at the edge of the known world. I would be the dragon on that map. "May I see it?"

"I left it in the car," he said. "Mind if I smoke?"

"I'd rather you didn't."

"People usually say they don't mind even when they do. I ought to commend you for being honest." He shrugged off his parka and handed it to me. His yellow turtleneck was tight and damp with sweat. He had eyebrows now.

"Why didn't you call first? I actually have a land-line here."

"I couldn't," he said. "I left directly from work, where I have *zero phone privileges.*"

"No cell phone?"

"It broke. There was a *pay* phone at some gas station, outdoors, the wind blowing on my bare fingers." His fingers were hidden, no elaborate gestures to illustrate the narrative. "I dialed directory assistance. They asked, 'What city?' and I said, 'I don't know,' and I hung up. What city is this?"

"There's no city here," I said. "Would you talk a little lower?"

"Is someone asleep?"

I said nothing.

"So the quarter slipped from my fingers and disappeared in the snow and I started to panic, but said to myself, 'Forget it. Just go. He's up there, never goes anywhere. He'll appreciate the company.'" He kept looking at me, eyes almost closed, the expression my former cat would assume when he wished to intimidate me. "Although, of course, he lied a little, covered up the fact that he's an artist. That he sells his work in galleries, makes a pretty good living from it."

I let those words float in the quiet. I did not live off the sale of my paintings. The best, the most valuable, I kept for myself, hidden upstairs.

"I got lost in Silver Lake," he said. "Not the lake itself, but the dinky little village."

"Did you consider the possibility that I might be busy, or not even home?"

"What?"

"You told me about your routine last summer—how you keep your brain going at the museum, guarding those ugly paintings?"

"I'm so impressed you remember. And that you're talking this much. I'm bowled over." He traced an eyebrow with one finger. "I rehearsed things to say, most of which I've forgotten. Now I'm making it up as I go."

"I see."

"I wanted to ask about work. How's the job situation up here?"

"No jobs. It's a ghost town. Not even a town." I finally sat down, on a twig chair I had finished in September. Already the chair was shaping itself to my body, and I took pleasure from that. At least one part of my body felt good. I craved a hot drink, but any form of self-indulgence would wait until later. Yes, there were jobs around here, but not for him.

"A ghost town?"

"It's typical Adirondacks. All the locals are unemployed during the winter, except the woman who delivers my propane and plows my driveway." Cindy. Short for Cynthia.

"I'd pump gas," he said. "Really. I would do anything. I could be a caretaker."

"Aren't you somewhat overqualified for pumping gas?"

"I resent people saying that to me. Like everything is ruled out. Everything. Don't you have friends with places like this, who need a caretaker?"

"No." A place like this. Sure, on an island in the middle of Silver Lake, a place that stayed empty all winter. Elise was there only three months of the year, could afford a caretaker for the other nine months.

"Okay, I said I would pump gas. Where should I apply?"

"The fact is, Bruce, you'd have to be a local even to get the worst jobs. And then you'd have to wait in line ten years for somebody to die or move south. Just to pump gas. Caretaker jobs are inherited."

"Keep talking," he said.

"Okay," I said. "Believe whatever you want." This was not going to be easy. He would stay until I ordered him to leave. Subtle suggestions would not do the job.

"What about fast food?" he said. "I'd work in a Burger King. I'd mop the floor. Clean the toilets."

"No fast food in town, not in winter. Dairy Freeze in Cedar Lake is all we have and it shuts down the day after Labor Day. It may never reopen. For sale."

"Okay, so I'd live here and commute to a larger town." He gestured with one hand, pointing. He had short, clean fingernails now. Perhaps he *could* pump gas, scrub floors, but his hand pointed in the wrong direction, northwest, where there were no towns for sixty miles. Nothing. "I think one of your light bulbs just burned out," he said.

"Live here?" I asked. "What do you mean by 'here?'"

"Here. I could rent one of your outbuildings. One of the five or six."

"They're unheated."

"I'm not particular. I'd live in a tent if I had to. I'd live in an outhouse. My car is a twenty-year-old piece of junk, but I'd commute. Two hours each way wouldn't kill me." He seemed very eager. His eyes were bright, eyebrows hopeful.

"There might be jobs within two hours of here." I should have said there weren't any, turned off the lights, doused the fire, kicked him out the door. Literally.

"How about something for a museum guard? Two years' experience, reliable, well-educated?"

"The Adirondack Museum is closed all winter—the only real museum within two hours."

"A long shot, anyway."

"The only kind of guards we have up here in winter are prison guards." I looked at him—too thin, too weak to guard even an ugly painting.

"They have *prisons* up here?"

"The main industry. At least five prisons within two hours of this lake. Federal, state, minimum security, shock camps for youthful offenders, country club prisons for tax cheaters. You name it. They might need more guards."

"You're so indirect about everything, which you confuse with being polite. You know what I mean?"

I shrugged.

"You don't really want me up here."

"I didn't say that."

"I wish you would."

I closed my eyes. I felt the heat from the fire, mostly on my knees. My throat was parched but the special drink could wait—warm and sweet, spiked with rum, a sprinkle of cinnamon or nutmeg. I would make it last until bedtime. The comforter in my bedroom was thick but light and always smelled good, as if lined with balsam. I had a top-of-the-line hot-water bottle, which I would fill after he left. There were many comforting little steps to go through before retiring for the evening.

"The smoke from the fire is nice, but I could really use a cigarette."

"I don't smoke," I said. "You should have stopped at the store."

"The store?"

"Silver Lake. Open all year. You can stop and get your tank filled on your way back to the city. Expensive. Actually, you could have stopped there first, bought your cigarettes, filled your tank, then given me a call. They have my number."

"Could have, or *should* have?"

"I only talk about possibilities. Not obligations."

"Bullshit." He stood up and moved toward the fireplace, hugging himself tightly, his arms so long that his hands nearly met across his lower back, as if another person, also a fingernail-biter, were hugging him. He inspected the watercolor above the mantel—lake and mountain and red canoe, intricate patterns of waves. One of a series. It had my signature on it, an illegible scribble protecting my identity from the overly curious. Next to it was the "map painting," an enlargement of the map I had drawn for the loon count two years earlier. The loons were now almost life-size. The lake water was the most brilliant blue.

This person in my house—merely an *art guard*—had no business talking about the art itself, and might very well get into trouble if he speculated about the artist's intent, his real life, his minor scandals. Such an artist's life, fully known, would be red meat to a person like him. He had probably hoped for a tour of the house. I thought of *Martha*, the painting upstairs—sometimes covered with a baby blue bedsheet, but not right now. That would be something: Bruce staring at it, not necessarily with prurient interest, but definitely wanting the backstory. A good story, but only Martha and I knew it. Her soon-to-be-ex had a general idea.

It started after she bought the *Canoe at Sunset* painting on display at the town museum. Five thousand dollars! I asked her, "What can I do for you?" I felt as if I owed her. "You mean, to make me happy?" And the whole affair took a while. By "affair," I mean the creation of the nude portrait, although there was also an affair on the side, not conducted here—Russ and Linda would have noticed—nor in Martha's Silver Lake camp. I never visited her camp. Her husband was there "all the time." No, we would get our coffees at the store, separately, and drive south past the LEAVING ADIRONDACK PARK sign, and meet at a motel near the Thruway. The Adirondack Motel, a half hour south of the Blue Line, "not very Adirondack," Martha kept saying. I brought along my sketch pad and pastels, and Martha posed for me in the motel room. It took three months to get it right, stretching into the cold months of October and November. "Don't you have to go back to the city to work?" I asked her. "Work?" she said. "I don't have to work."

When the painting was finished, she told me to keep it. "For now." And then there was the time when my parents popped in while Martha was visiting. (After all, it was still their camp.) My mother said she had tried to call, but it kept going to voicemail and the robot voice kept saying the mailbox was full, so they drove up from their place in the city (a two-hour drive) to do a "welfare check," and when they saw I already had company, they went out in the rowboat for an hour, came back, kissed me good-bye—both of them. The next day, my mother called. I picked up right away, and she said, "We were so relieved!" About what? "She's beautiful. We were so worried. There you were, not married, thirty-three years old, and we had no idea what was going on in your life. We were worried you might never be happy," and so on. I told her I wasn't all that happy, and she kept going on about how beautiful Martha was, as if her beauty were all that mattered. The last thing my mother said was, "Elise called and wondered why you didn't do the loon count this year." Because I was busy.

"What time is it?" Bruce asked.

"Three-thirty." I could tell the approximate time from the angle of light coming through the front window. Nine winters in the same place had taught me how. I had no clocks in the house, never wore a watch.

"You must have gotten off work *really early* this morning," I said, "if it took you seven hours to drive here. Do they have a night shift at the museum? I suppose they would need guards at night. Armed guards."

"I didn't go to work today." He continued to examine the red canoe in the picture above the mantel, squinting as if to discover a small and telling detail, as if he expected to find himself seated in that canoe, alone, or with me—which would have given him the right to stay with me forever—in the main house, no less. But I hadn't even put Russ and Linda in the canoe. I had painted an empty red canoe drifting across the lake, away from my camp, the slightest ripple of wave to show which direction it moved—a motif I liked, repeated in several paintings.

"Was it a holiday?" I asked. "One of your days off?"

"No."

"Then what was it?"

"I don't work in that jail anymore. I had a fight with my boss. She caught me asleep, leaning against the wall. Actually, my shoulder accidentally bumped the edge of some awful ten-million-dollar painting and set off an alarm. I was a little drunk, but they didn't give me a breath test." He shrugged his shoulders, stepped away from my wall. "We had an argument and then she told me to turn in my uniform and get the hell out. Everything I own is in my car."

I said nothing.

"It's so quiet here. Any little alarm bell ringing in a stupid museum more than two hundred miles away in the city is totally irrelevant up here. The entire population of New York City could scream in unison, 'Bruce touched the painting!' and you wouldn't hear a peep."

And then my mother phoned while Bruce was still visiting. She opened with "I'm so glad you answered right away." I'm Johnny-on-the-spot. "Are you staying warm, Wesley?" Yes, of course, I have a nice fire going. "Speaking of which, have you checked all the batteries in the smoke alarms?" Yes, of course, all ten of them. "Don't be sarcastic. You know that was a serious question." Yes, Mother, I checked them. "That's better," she said. "Is there anyone there with you?" I said nothing, but Bruce heard the question and shouted, "*I'm* here!," to which my mother replied, "That voice didn't sound like you, Wesley." *It's just a friend, Mother.* A long pause followed. "Now you've got me worrying again." I'll call you back tomorrow, Mom, okay? "But you never do," she said.

So now she was worried about me. Actually, I kind of liked it. And there was very little chance of a "welfare check" in January, no pop in. They were in Florida.

The room grew darker. We didn't talk for a while. The fire made enough noise. We sat and looked at it, reading into the fire our separate thoughts. Who was this guy? *Bruce.* I had forgotten. It seemed like a decent enough name, nothing to be afraid of, possibly the name of a guy who fit in well among the scattered residents of a community, a guy who did good works, kept the lines of communication open, breathed life into a dead town, ran a nice little gallery, set up a simple concert series, encouraged his artist friends to move to the Adirondacks. If a local kid had come to me, in the middle of winter, asking for a job, I would have hired him. But no local kid would ever have been so bold.

"You're very lucky," Bruce finally said. "It's perfect here."

"Getting dark. No motels nearby. Hardly any light left. Did you bring a flashlight with you?"

"I thought *you'd* have one. Why would I need a flashlight? Are you putting me in an outbuilding?"

I went to the triple window. Zero-degree cold radiated through the glass. The dock and boathouse were covered in snow. I was happy to be on the inside. I thought about what Bruce had said earlier, that a person could stock up on food and not go out at all, live like a hermit, let it snow and never plow the driveway. The only people who would know I existed would be cross-country skiers coming down the lake, who would notice the light in my studio, at dusk. They might figure it was nothing more than the reflection of the sun setting.

"It gets dark fast up here, Bruce," I said. "All those mountains block the late afternoon light, what there is of it. Very depressing." The faint band of salmon light seemed colder than any blue.

"Oh, I'm not affected by that. What do they call it?" He snapped his fingers. "Seasonal affective disorder. I don't mind darkness. I can adjust. My theory is, where you are and who you are with is much more important than the amount of sunlight in the sky. People who buy those fancy fluorescent light box things and sit inside them, they aren't going to solve their problems." He could live with darkness. He could live with anything—bad job, isolation, sub-zero weather, my hostility. He said he could live in an outhouse. I might have to kill him to get rid of him.

I put on my fur-lined parka, pulled a green plaid scarf out of the pocket, and wrapped it around my neck. Kept my wool ski cap on. "Sometimes I get depressed," I said. "And I stop talking."

"I'm comfortable, really comfortable. You made a very nice fire for me."

"I've done better."

"Do you have a bathroom in this palace?"

"Down the hall and to the left. Bucks and Does."

The light was gone from the triple window, the last bit of salmon pink. Nothing but blackness out there. I imagined an army of intruders moving through the dark toward my place. While he used the lavatory (one of five on the property), I considered the motives of my friends, Russ and Linda. Why had they dumped this person on me last summer and then given him a map so he could drive to my place and bother me in the middle of winter? The summer motive I came up with was plausible: they needed their privacy in their three-room camp, if only for a couple of hours of intimacy. Here's what I figured: earlier this winter, he had visited *them* unannounced, and this visit to my place was a form of punishment. *Go bother Wesley!* Winter—it made no sense. He lived in Manhattan; they lived in Utica. No need to dump him on me. Was this a trick?

"You're right," he said, emerging from the hall-way that led to the closest lavatory. "I should have called first. A phone call would have been a lot more three-dimensional than this. This is hardly even two-dimensional. You know what I mean? Why are you dressed to go outside?"

I held out his boots toward him. My hands shook a little. "I think they've warmed up enough." I stuck my hand in one boot, then pulled it out, and touched his hand with it. "Nice and warm. Ready to put on, Bruce."

"My job was like a prison, anyway. 'No slouching.' Punch the clock." He kept complaining about his miserable job. "Are you listening, man?"

I gauged the light, how colors faded into gray. When, exactly, did color become only a memory of color?

"But anyway," he said, "I stood there like a robot and planned my day, what I would pick up at the market, how much change I'd get back from a twenty, how I would cook my supper. I timed everything and laid everything out precisely. The place settings, the exact arrangement. Do you ever live that way?"

I shook my head very slightly.

"You don't?"

"I eat when I'm hungry, go to bed when I'm tired." *Paint when I feel like it*, I said to myself. If I mentioned painting, he would never stop talking.

"You're trying to make your life sound boring, aren't you?"

I shook my head.

"Why are you dressed to go out?" he asked again. "I'm sorry, are you going out on a date with someone?"

"No."

"Are you cold? It's warm in here. Take off your coat."

He moved toward the other side of the room. On the wall, above an antique rolltop desk, hung a painting of Whiteface Mountain, in photo-realistic style, its snowy top reflecting the last inch of a winter sunset.

"Very nice," he said.

"It's an original."

"Who's the artist?"

"A local."

"All right," he said. "I'll put my boots on before they get cold." He took the boots from me. He stuck his foot in the left boot. He stopped for a moment and said, "Although I can picture myself walking barefoot up your driveway. A half mile, barefoot in the snow."

"It's two hundred yards. Very cold out there."

"Barefoot. That would be interesting. What do you think?" He shook the other boot at me. "Let's imagine it, step-by-step, out to the highway. Can *you* picture it? Could you eventually make art out of it? You could certainly paint the landscape, but could you put in the person?"

"Don't do it."

"Why not? What do you care?" His eyebrows still had a hopeful arch to them, but the rest of his face had lost all hope.

The next morning, the rising sun woke me at 8:30. Pancakes and coffee. I put on my coat and hat and walked the grounds of the estate, following the small footprints out toward the highway where he had parked his car, footprints so small and light they could have been animal tracks. Evidently he had tiptoed most of the way in his bare feet, and then put on the boots. I had not walked to the car with him. I had watched from the back porch, then stepped inside. At certain points, I could see that he had stopped, walked in small circles, as if looking at a valuable object. As if he had been playing out the future, rehearsing his footsteps, the way he would stand and turn—wherever he ended up, whatever he was guarding.

My mother called later in the day. "Is he still there?" she asked.

"Who?"

"The man who was visiting you when I called."

"And I had you worried."

"I guess I'm not worried now," she said, tentatively, "not to the extent that I'll spend another sleepless night. Less worried, but still worried."

The Hiker

Four times that August morning Joan had driven past the young man. He hadn't moved except to do a deep knee bend, which he held for a second, then straightened up. Thumb out, he stood along the edge of Route 10B—the wild stretch north of Silver Lake where the power lines disappeared into the ground—a hitchhiker in his twenties, possibly younger, wearing a bright green ball cap and a full-size pack, the kind you'd take on a long hike. Whoever had dropped him off had failed to pick him up. Signals crossed, a sad outcome, now dependent on the kindness of Joan, or another driver.

Joan felt guilty about making so many back-and-forth trips—twelve miles of highway between her property and the Silver Lake store, but the day was hot and she'd forgotten the ice for the cooler. She always kept a gallon jug of spring water in a cooler, which she would pour over her head at the end of an afternoon of splitting firewood, then rub her head with a frayed green towel from the ragbag. No beach, no shower, completely off-grid—much less complicated than being right on the lake. A fine-looking driveway curved artfully around the edge of the knoll, paved with crushed stone (two loads' worth), bordered by well-placed rocks, giving the impression that the driveway led to a beautiful vacation home. It led, in fact, to an 8 x 10 platform with a tent on it, a beige glamping tent. Further up the hill was a comfortable outhouse, almost as large as the tent, and more permanent. From there, a path led to a cleared half acre where Joan grew squash and tomatoes and dreamed of setting up an array of solar panels. On hot days, she threw melted ice from the cooler at the plants, and they thrived. At last count, she had forty-three little green tomatoes, and twice as many blossoms. Countless squash.

She was on her way back to the store to buy a can of mosquito repellant, and an "after-bite" dispenser, if they had any. Or witch hazel, much cheaper. Her ankles itched along the sock line, which distracted her, impaired her judgment. She also wanted to buy the *Gazette*, for the daily puzzle.

The hitchhiker held a hand-lettered cardboard sign. It read, CITY.

Joan parked her Volvo on the highway shoulder, rolled down the window.

"What city?" she asked.

"Any city," the young man said, with a slight lisp, and tossed his gear into the back seat. Joan had never said, "Get in." Had never said, "Okay, I'll take you anywhere on the planet"—though stopping for this hitchhiker implied a willingness on her part, a sense of adventure, and poor judgment. This hitchhiker had emerged from the wilderness. That he had emerged alone should have meant something, beyond mere stupidity. Joan had a soft spot in her heart for hitchhikers, from when she was in her twenties, hitchhiking out West, not reckless, really, but curious about how things might turn out, especially if she accepted a ride from a stranger. Or, as a driver, offered a ride.

Last summer, she had even given a ride to Monty LeBeau. She had seen him a few miles south of her place on the same route, picking up cigarette butts from the side of the road and stashing them in a fanny pack. Nothing had happened in the car, just a dull conversation about poachers on his property. His mother's property. People in the store told Joan never to give him a ride again. "He's crazy." And so was *she!* they seemed to imply.

This hitchhiker with the CITY sign looked normal, younger than Monty, in much better physical condition, nicely outfitted. His backpack could not have weighed more than five pounds, the way he tossed it, and the way it landed, with a light bounce. A legitimate heavy pack would have crushed Joan's empty plastic jugs.

"I recognize you," the young man said without looking at her.

"What?"

"The car. I saw you driving back and forth all morning, trying to make up your mind."

"Maybe," Joan said. "Once or twice. But it had nothing to do with you." She was driving south. There were no cities to the north, hardly a village, until you got to Canada. "Just my own lack of planning," she continued. "If I weren't so lazy, I'd be doing this back-and-forth thing on a bicycle. And you'd be out of a ride. Do I sound heartless?"

"I'd like a bicycle. I bet you have more than one bicycle."

"I'll drop you off at the store in Silver Lake, as far as I'm going today. Not much of a 'city,' but you can make a call from there. It's on the grid." She didn't have a bicycle on her property, only a blueprint in her head for a small building in which to stash a bicycle. Maybe one of those Amish-built garden sheds from Broome County. She kept her bicycles in a large closet back in the city.

"I got nobody to call," the young man said. He cranked his window down an inch.

"Looks like you've been in the woods a few days. Deer flies pretty bad?"

"That's like asking me, 'Do you breathe air?'"

"Excuse me?"

"Which is what my dad once asked me, for no good reason, except maybe to imply that I came from another planet. He doesn't ask me stupid questions anymore. But I'm starting to figure out what he meant. He never thought I was normal, or even human. Maybe he was a little scared of me. 'Don't sit behind me,' he'd say, when we rode in the car. 'I should put you in handcuffs,' was another thing he liked to say, if it was just me and him in the car."

Joan didn't own handcuffs. Or rope. She had an unhealthy trust in strangers, an expectation that she might learn something from them if she asked the right questions. What she should have learned over the years was to trust *no one*. "I'm ready for you to tell me about the hike," she said. "How long were you in the woods? Discover any new mountains?"

They passed an enclave of private land, the visible part cluttered with junked cars and trucks and vans, even a rusted bulldozer. A month ago Joan had waved at the owner, a bearded Walt Whitman type, who jumped into the road and waved back, a huge gesture that seemed to mean *Stop!* Joan had not stopped, only swerved and tapped the brakes slightly.

"A complicated question," the young man finally said.

"What question?" Then Joan remembered and said, "Oh, it's not complicated. You could answer in three or four words."

"But you'd think I was an idiot," he said.

"Try me. We've only got fifteen minutes, and then you'll stop having to worry about what I think of you."

"Why should I worry about that?" *He is an idiot. He just contradicted himself.*

"I was kidding," Joan said.

"I never worry about what people think of me," the young man said.

"Very good," Joan said.

"You don't either, do you? I can tell from looking at you."

Wow. What was it? Was it her face? It could have been the old cancer surgery scars on her right cheek, where she'd been scraped twice, decades ago—which might have looked as if she'd been in a fight with a black bear. Maybe the fact that she wore no makeup. Was it her uncombed blond-and-gray hair? She was in the wilderness. At work in the city, she would make an effort, but even there her appearance didn't seem to matter. She was invisible. She had always been invisible, and unwilling to do whatever might have made her more visible. Many friends; no lovers. Now, she had a man in the car, noticing her, drawing conclusions about her.

She drifted to the shoulder to let a tailgating pickup pass, the way she often did along this quarter-mile stretch of highway.

"You dumping me here?"

"No, of course not," she said. "Too far from civilization." Meaning, *the store.*

The rough pavement dated from the early 1980s, never patched. The State of New York had forgotten this part of the Adirondacks. Joan didn't care what they did with this road. It could revert to gravel. It would still be the most beautiful place in the world. Each modest turnoff with a TRAILHEAD PARKING sign offered visible splendor just a few steps beyond the parking area. Briefly, she turned her head to check whether anyone had parked at her favorite turnoff, with its short trail to a secret ledge where she liked to sit and watch the birds and meditate on things like her reputation. How her cousins would say things like, "Joan, you need to take better care of yourself," as if her lifestyle were a constant tempting of fate. Carolyn once said, "Are you trying to kill yourself?" A rhetorical question. Neither "yes" nor "no" would have been a satisfactory answer, although "no" was the true answer. She wasn't suicidal.

No one had parked at her favorite spot.

"You know," the hitchhiker said, "when we get to the store and I pick up the phone, there won't be anybody to call. Maybe the store could give me a job. I'd work for food."

"They're pretty much fully staffed for the summer."

"How would you know?"

"My cousin owns it." A second cousin, once removed. She had cousins scattered all over the southern Adirondacks, though Joan herself had not been born nor raised there. Originally a city girl, Catholic schools straight through from kindergarten to Le Moyne. And then a steady government job—not teaching, though she'd taken education courses in college. She didn't have the temperament.

"So you get a discount on everything? Free candy bars?"

"Hardly," Joan said. "I'll give you a situation. Let's say I paid two bucks for a jug of water and I have a bag of other stuff I have to carry out to the car first, and I leave the jug of water on the counter and drive away. It happens all the time, but I don't make a big fuss about it. I don't come back the next day trying to claim the jug of water I paid for. They probably put it back on the shelf. They could use the two-dollar profit, my cousin and her family. I never count my change. They always round up the price of their gasoline, ten cents more than the city. I don't complain. Life is good."

"So you're rich."

"No, I'm *not* rich."

"What they all say. Me, though, I'd do anything for minimum wage. Anything. I'd take less than minimum wage. I've been cut off at home."

"Cut off?" She wanted details.

"I thought I could just hike around and stuff, but that didn't exactly pan out."

"Tell me about the hike you just finished. I don't want to have to keep asking."

"I'm in a bad spot now," the kid said. "I have, like, seven cents in my pocket. If it hadn't been in my pocket, my father would have grabbed it away from me. *He cut me off.* But sometimes, he gives me all kinds of junk, to make up for things. I need a job."

Joan smiled, then said, "You could sit at the card table outside the Silver Lake general store on Sunday mornings and sell newspapers for them. Diane said they were looking for somebody."

The young man paused. "How much do they pay?"

"You'd be done before lunch and clear maybe twenty dollars. You gotta start somewhere."

"Before I end up nowhere. *This* is nowhere."

"It's the Adirondacks," Joan said. "Have a little re-spect." *Like, look out the window, young man, there's a sliver of blue, a lake that no one knows, a dead tree with a bald eagle perched on the highest branch, and that's only what we can see from the highway.*

"You're not my mother."

Joan smiled. She was no one's mother, although de-cades ago, in another life, she had unwillingly thrown away an opportunity. Adoption, not abortion. Absen-tee father, whereabouts unknown. She often thought about the child, now in his late thirties, walking around in the world, hiking, climbing, surviving. Joan was no one's wife, no one's sister. Everyone's cousin, it seemed.

"You don't know nothing about me," her passenger said. "Nothing!"

"True," Joan said. "Except, you have seven cents in your pocket. And your father cut you off. You might have been exaggerating."

"You talk too much."

"Hey, don't get hostile," she said. "I'm just the driver."

"You're a lot more than that," the young man said. He pulled out a knife and held it vertically, like a hitch-hiker's thumb. Small and rusty, but dangerous.

Joan nodded, having expected a knife, or maybe a gun—a small pistol tucked into the kid's belt. She kind of welcomed the knife, loosened her collar, her bare neck exposed.

Although in this moment the situation seemed dire, it was going to end the way *she* wanted it to end.

The thing about hikers: if they had the right look—overequipped and undernourished—Joan would do just about anything for them. Not like vagrants in the city, who would trespass through her backyard and make their demands. Hikers were different. She'd see them on the edge of the road, leaning against a tree, bedraggled, thirsty, feverish, or face down in the weeds, possibly epileptic. Struggling. They wouldn't have to signal their distress or hold up a sign; she would stop.

This young man holding a knife to her neck—she might turn him around before she was done with him.

There had been a long-distance hiker who became a friend for life, like an honorary nephew, who, while Joan drove him south to the city, told her to stop at a restaurant just north of the Blue Line, and then treated her to a thirty-dollar lunch. David—who'd just quit grad school, law school. He'd been living in the Shaker Mountain Wild Forest since early spring, living off a loaf of cheap white bread and a one-pound brick of Velveeta and sometimes gathering, along certain scrubby mountain ridges, wild blackberries and raspberries. He had aluminum foil folded in his pocket and dry matches, so that when he caught fish and snakes—by hand—he could make a meal out of them. He would eat wild spinach that looked more like poison ivy. After she parted with him, in the city, he kept in touch, describing his hikes—the solo journeys, mostly bushwhacking, into the heart of something greater than mountains, a young man oblivious to pain, starvation, malnutrition, deer flies, public opinion. A true stoic who had read philosophy, beyond college. The rest of the year (David never hiked in winter or spring) was a blank, an unwritten subject. He could have worked as a janitor or a security guard. It didn't matter. Joan understood completely. Until recently, she had been an office worker in a high-rise building, from which, on the highest floor, a few Adirondack peaks were visible on the clearest days, the southernmost range between Corinth and Lake George, enough to keep her dreaming.

A full-time commitment to the hiking life would have taken away all the meaning. A full-time commitment would have been insane. One needed another life, perhaps a paper-pushing life in the city, very different from the hiking life, from which the latter represented a significant deviation; and even if such a deviation could be enjoyed only one weekend per year, it was sufficient. There would always be more weekends coming.

If she lived. This time she may have risked too much.

"Are you nervous?" the young man asked.

"You don't need to hold that thing so close to my neck," Joan said. "I'd be perfectly happy to drive you wherever you want to go. I'm free the rest of the day. I was thinking of climbing the little hill behind my property, as long as the wind keeps blowing. Half-mile hike. It's a beauty. I marked it with red ribbon. You could hike—"

"I want you to stop *talking*." The young man emphasized the last word with a slight twinge and twist of the knife blade, not enough to draw blood, but close. Joan could smell body odor—like a mammal, a raccoon three days dead, an authentic hiking odor, acquired honestly.

She *would* turn him around, save him from himself. In five or ten minutes, she might speak again. Or she might keep her thoughts to herself. She moved her lips. Red signs with white lettering appeared at every turn: crawlers, soft ice cream, kerosene, canoes, cabins, etc.

"Look at those fat asses waddling into the store," the young man said. "I don't care if they're your friends and relatives. Your mother, even. Don't slow down. Don't honk. No weird signals. No good-bye kisses."

Couldn't this young man have humored her with details about the hike? Was it all mosquitoes and no views? Joan figured he had hidden behind a tree ten yards off the highway. A fake hiker. She savored the thought.

"My dad, though. If he could see me. Boy, oh boy."

Living out his father's dreams, or pretending to. Criminal dreams.

"'Be prepared,' he liked to say. 'Always bring a knife.' But my dad was no Boy Scout."

Church. Joan wanted to say it out loud. If the kid had gone to church, instead of the mountains, he'd be different. Or if he'd read a book. She had a copy of *Into the Wild* somewhere on the back seat, under the water jugs. Reading a good book would set him straight, give him a context. Hikes weren't supposed to end this way, with threats and intimidation.

"You're driving too slow," he said. "Twenty on the curves? Stop daydreaming. Stop trying to change what's happening, lady. You got plenty of gas in the tank, the needle ain't moving. Pee your pants, I don't care. Hold it in, like I do. I peed all over the woods, the past few days. At least I brought enough water with me. Or almost enough. I drank out of a footprint once or twice. I stuck my face in it, an inch of dirty water, and sucked it between my teeth. I guess you can live a week on muddy water, but maybe after a while, you get delusional."

Exactly.

The young man's grip on the knife relaxed. Joan tried to rotate her neck, just a fraction of an inch. "I felt that," the young man said. "You think I'm tired, but I'm wide awake, biting my tongue and sucking blood. You might think I'm going to fall asleep right now and you can dump me by the side of the road." The knife blade wobbled slightly. "Maybe you slept in a nice bed last night. I slept on a rock. I had a rock for a pillow."

Bad breath. Not just mammal stink. Joan would have given him a stick of peppermint gum, fed him a decent meal. She was known for her generosity. She once treated Monty to a home-cooked meal. *Don't do that again*, her cousins said.

"I kind of liked it," the young man continued. "Having a rock for a pillow."

Uh-huh.

"I pushed over a tree. It was dying anyway."

Uh-huh.

"You couldn't see the leaves until the tree was laid out on the ground. They were green. Shaped like a star." He went on and on. Like a child. Hopeless.

To cover such ramblings, Joan kept a song going in her head, written by an old guy in Kentucky—a friend of a friend. Something about a deer.

"I don't really want to go to the city today," the passenger said. "The city's too big. Forget it. The city was a horror movie."

The song actually began with a lament about noise in the city. The song was dated, mourning the imminent extinction of Canada geese and white-tailed deer, both of which had become Adirondack pests. The song might have been written in the 1970s, when people believed what Joan's friend Robert called "that eco-bullshit."

"When we get to the next road, I'll tell you where to turn," the passenger said. "I'll tell you where to keep going straight, go left, go right. This is a lot easier than the damn trails, where the signs are, like, mostly torn down or broken off or never existed. Piles of rocks with no meaning."

Cairns. With plenty of meaning.

"Too many trees getting in the way. A trap, is what I think." He paused, breathed hard and said, "Maybe you should just dump me." His voice cracked on the last two words.

Not ready to do that, Joan thought.

"Traps everywhere."

Not yet.

"Like, three years ago my dad takes me to EMS in Saratoga—Eastern Mountain Sports, right?—and he says, 'Whatever you need, you pick it out, doesn't matter how much.' Unbelievable. All of a sudden he's not treating me like a piece of shit. I could have gone nuts in that place. But I don't really like the outdoors. Seriously. I just picked things at random that didn't even cost two hundred dollars, and when I put on my gear at home, my dad said, 'Now you really look like somebody.' Exactly what he said. He doesn't know who I am. He can read about it in the paper. It'll be in the paper, right?"

Joan said nothing, as if gagged.

"You can talk now, if you want. Talk!"

Joan still said nothing.

"The newspaper in hell is the one he reads now. It wasn't me, but it could have been. We came real close. Worse than this." His voice kept getting higher, spiraling into child-like wonder. "I'm gonna carve my name in something huge, so he knows it's me, and not some other crazy hiker. It's me, Dad." The kid laughed, a nervous whinny.

It's me, Dad. Good line.

"Hey, lady. Why are you smiling?"

The answer was complicated. She would have to talk too much, and she was done with talking, done with asking questions, giving advice, all that crap. Where had it ever gotten her? Her cousins and friends only gave advice; they never took any.

The car went over a bump, and something made a hollow sound on the back seat—the empty backpack. The young man said, "Whoa. Slow down, lady."

Joan, of course, said nothing. After a few minutes of silence, the knife dropped away from her neck. She wanted to say something. She touched her neck, then looked at her finger. No blood. She breathed deeply, then coughed, fake-coughed, to get a reaction. She was controlling things now.

"Are we lost?" the hiker asked, sleepily.

Not exactly, not literally.

Well, *he* was lost, but Joan knew the geography very well, and how she would use it, and how it would end this story. They were about to descend the last hill leading out of the Adirondacks, toward a "city," fifteen miles distant. Joan knew a side road, paved—albeit narrowing and breaking apart—a road curving back into the wilderness, almost imperceptibly, into a trackless region of small lakes and stunted mountains and slight, unmarked openings just visible from the road, vague openings that turned into excellent hiking trails after a few hundred yards—some of them—curving away from swamps into a second-growth forest of hemlock and beech and yellow birch, the trees last harvested so long ago the rotted stumps had worn away.

She turned the car around at an old trailhead, where the road briefly widened. "Get out," she said, and the hiker obeyed. "And take your empty pack." He obeyed, and appeared briefly in her rearview mirror, a crumbling assemblage of geometric shapes—such an unlikely hiker, an abstraction, like the generic hiker on a road sign. Finally, she lost sight of him.

Joan wasn't sure of her destination. She didn't feel like hiking. Maybe a very short walk. She considered her favorite turnoff a few minutes south of her property, the small parking area with a clear view from the ledge, a few acres of open water—a good place to stop and think about what this experience had meant, and to tamp down the bad memories it had evoked. *No*, she said to herself, *that was almost forty years ago, you don't have to go through that, don't touch your neck, that's not how he did it, there's no feeling left, not even from the knife that fell away less than an hour ago.*

A solitary loon had landed on the open water. A mistake. She began talking to it. "I can't help you, dear. There are a dozen other lakes where you could land, not far from here. You don't have a long enough runway here for takeoff, you'll have a problem when it freezes up in a few months. You'll never leave. Did anyone count you last month?"

On Giant Mountain

Summer of 1977, her hike. Summer of 1997, my hike.
As if our notes in the trailhead register formed a con-
tinuity. As if—through trail notes, years apart—one
could form a kind of kinship.

This was the story Regina could have told me, and
I might have believed it: She had hiked Giant in the
dark, without a flashlight. She liked to say I had caught
her in my arms when she tumbled off a cliff. Really?
When she paused for a deep breath, in the telling of
this story, I asked, "How high was the cliff?" and she
said, "Oh, Robert, high enough so I could yell, 'One
Mississippi, two Mississippi' and still have time for a
quick prayer before you caught me." But her adventure
actually happened—if it happened at all—while I was
elsewhere, tent camping with my parents in some tame
area of the western Adirondacks, under strict rules for
mealtimes and bedtimes. That long-ago summer Regina had rambled, unsupervised, from high peak to
high peak, without a tent or a sleeping bag, living on
bread and cheese and pure stream water. She would

hike with anyone—Boy Scout troops, wanderers, strange men in their thirties.

I once saw her feed a live mouse to a snake—in her bedroom, in the cottage next to the store, the summer she worked there. But for the rest of it—the weird hike on Giant Mountain—I wasn't there. I had to take her word for it and fill in the blanks.

Maybe the truth was in the poems she sent, poems I burned after reading. The truth might very well have been in those poems.

Right now, decades later, I'm spending eight months out of the year in my grandfather's cabin on Silver Lake, only a half mile from the store where I used to hang out and play my guitar, where people would throw money—big bills sometimes—into my guitar case, thinking I was poor, if not actually talented. My own story of climbing Giant is also an old one, though not nearly as old as Regina's.

You see the south face of Giant from the road and it scares you. You flinch, step hard on the brakes. But this thing is even more terrifying than it looks. The cliffs, smoothed out by distance and poor eyesight, are tucked into the center, the part that occasionally breaks apart in a storm and sends landslides onto Route 73.

"Hike down ahead of me," she must have said to the guy who actually hiked with her, in the near dark. "In case I fall off a cliff."

"I'll catch you," he answered. He reached out and grabbed her around the waist, and for a second they danced on the mountain. He was a lot older: I imagine a bread truck driver with a wife and children at home, but from a distance it looked okay. He was trim, with a full head of black hair. From a distance he could have been her age.

She kissed him. "We should hold hands all the way down."

"Where is everybody?"

An open ridge stretched almost to the summit, miles of rock, exposed and dry, gray-blue, dappled white, trespassing on the innocent sky. One time when I climbed Giant, I did it without a canteen. Near the top, desperately parched, I scooped dirty water out of a boot print and rinsed my mouth. Regina wasn't with me. No, Regina never hiked with me. By the time I got serious about doing the High Peaks, she had entered a new phase of her high-risk life—a cult religion, a downstate commune, a gig in California dancing topless in a cage.

And so I did what the Adirondack Mountain Club strongly advises hikers never to do, a prohibition listed as rule number one in the margin of any High Peaks map: "Do not hike alone." In this version of the climb, I'm doing it again. The fact of the matter is, I'm not alone. There will be dozens of climbers on a perfect day like this, mobs of them. Disabled along the trail, lying in the scrub pine, moaning, I will certainly be noticed, reported to the authorities, rescued, maybe even snatched from a remote cliff by a helicopter. The line of cars has already begun to form along the shoulder of the highway. Both sides. Twenty cars. The guidebook advises parking so the tires are completely off the pavement. A door swings out, almost whacks my fender. On Round Mountain, across Chapel Pond, people are climbing the rock face, yelling instructions that echo many times.

She would have hitched a ride to the trailhead—back then. Why did Regina and this older guy climb Giant Mountain so late in the day? Were they lost? She would say, "You can't get lost on this mountain! I mean, it's all so obvious! There's the top and there's the bottom, and look at all the ways they're connected." Yet this time around, only a half mile into the hike, I find myself in trouble, bushwhacking through the state-designated campsite south of the Giant's Washbowl, looking for an ATIS trail marker, or something better, an official sign with words pointing me toward the obvious summit.

Afterward, in the dark, they swam naked in Chapel Pond—which sounds inappropriate given the name of the pond, although it must happen all the time, hikers more inhibited than Regina, but so exhausted and dirty they have ceased to care about the highway traffic only a few yards away.

Regina and her hiking partner dined on rancid subs bought two days earlier in Schroon Lake. The mayo had gone bad, the turkey was never quite right, the lettuce had shriveled, and the Italian dressing did not kill the bacteria. So the late start was partly caused by food poisoning. Not by bad water—there was no bad water in the Adirondacks during that decade. Or no *fear* of bad water.

"Let's climb it anyway," she said, after vomiting. "I mean, we're here! Only three miles."

"What happened to the sun?"

"I think I swallowed it."

"The sun went down," the man said. "Getting dark now. Is it legal to hike in the dark?"

"I'll race you to the top. Last one up is a rotten egg."

They wore sneakers. Carried two packs of Cryst O Mints and no other food. There would be blueberries on the ridge between Giant Mountain and Rocky Peak Ridge, ripe and ready. Wild raspberries. Everything in this life would be laid out for them, Regina claimed. "Trust me." Indeed, she expected to meet up with other hikers who had carried too much food and water, who would gladly share, if only to lighten their loads.

In my daypack—for my solo hike, which takes place years later; I've turned sixty—I carry a single-serving Freihofer's apple pie, two no-name brownies, three plastic bottles of water, a hunk of Cabots seriously sharp cheddar cheese, stone-ground wheat crackers, a first-aid kit, unbreakable flashlight, face towel, trail guide with a map, a bag of peppermint candy, bug dope, after-bite, disposable camera, a foil tarp (although I have not camped overnight in decades), and my wallet, which, if I carried it in my pants pocket, would fall out on the trail. The first person they notify of my death or disappearance will smile and say, *That damn fool hiked alone.*

At the junction where the trail to Nubble veers to the left, the stream looks and sounds tasty, but I won't risk it. I dip my hat in the deepest part, then slap it back on my head. The suede bill is soaked, the water dribbling into my nose as I walk. The water could wreck the suede.

My cap cost twenty-five bucks. I wear it to keep the deer flies off my bald spot.

I should have clipped my toenails. It will be murder descending this mountain, my toes jammed into the end of the boot. Murder on the knees if I jump the slightest distance. Murder on the back. That is why I cannot imagine falling from a cliff, or being the person who catches the one who falls. I would certainly break apart, whether falling or catching.

"Barefoot," she told her partner, an excited whisper into his ear. I picture this clearly, though it was dark. *I hear it.*

"Not me."

"Well, *I'll* do it." She took off her sneakers and placed them in the middle of the trail, one on top of the other like a sort of cairn, a guidepost for the confused.

"I won't carry you."

"I could carry *you*," she said. "I'm just as big. Bigger. Look at my muscles."

"Can't see a thing."

"Barefoot is great. Totally naked would be better."

Across the valley, the sun had disappeared behind Dix Mountain. The residual glow sharply defined the steep edges of Elk Pass. By now, all other hikers were off the mountain, sitting by a lowland campfire, snuggled into a motel room. Home. To a hiker, home is a relative thing. The car looks like home. Or a human footprint on the trail. Even a candy wrapper.

"This is crazy," he said. "I might go to jail."

"Hey, if it gets too bad we'll just find a level place and stretch out, sleep until morning. Nobody is waiting up for us, right? Every human being who could worry about me knows absolutely nothing about this hike and wouldn't care even if they did know. My mother thinks I'm sulking in my bedroom. My father never thinks about me, whoever he is."

From the open ledge, they could see the lights of St. Huberts. Home was far away, beyond the very curvature of the earth.

She pinched him. "Least of all, your stupid wife." Yes, in this version of the hike, as I imagine it, the man is cheating on his wife.

The map is wet and smells like bug dope mixed with cheap sunscreen. "Giant Mountain Wilderness" is a rough triangle bounded by Route 73 on the west, 9N on the north, 9 on the east. I can cover the triangle with my hand, rub the wet brown contours into an ambiguous blur and turn this three-dimensional monster into a two-dimensional abstraction. In fact, as I climb, I hardly notice what I'm doing. The mountain is subsumed below sedimentary layers of thoughts, misgivings, aborted plans, faces of people I will never meet again.

Downhill hikers nod at me as they pass, but seldom say more than "howdy." They must have started out from the trailhead at sunrise.

"Nice on top?" I ask.

"Yeah," they answer. They could stretch it to ten words, encourage me with a lie—*Fifteen minutes and you'll hit the top. You're almost there. You can eat your lunch up there. The view is great, well worth the final push.*

For all their enthusiasm they could have stayed home and climbed this mountain with their fingers, traced the broken black lines on the map. In reality, the hash marks are painted yellow across the exposed rock face, nine inches long and two inches wide, sometimes scuffed out. These hikers count them. To speak with me would cause them to lose count.

The summit? I could settle for halfway up—the view is already splendid. I'm not bagging a peak. I'll never climb all forty-six. The thought of scrambling up Allen Mountain, or Seymour—or any of those trailless, viewless lumps with no claim to importance except their elevation above four thousand feet—depresses me. What is the point? There's a number ten can on top of Dipshit Mountain, with a notebook in it where you write your name to prove nothing more than the probability that you have lost your mind. The way I document my hikes, if only to assist my own failing memory, is to take photos of my daypack in various strategic positions—hanging from a dead tree next to a sign at the summit, sprawled next to a benchmark or against the front of a lean-to, profiled against the distinct horizon that is the reality of any mountain. "Gothics, as seen from Giant," the caption might read. Most summers it has been enough to catch a two-second glimpse of the High Peaks from Route 30 south of Indian Lake, not from the official turnoff, where the view looks out to the southeast and a mundane sequence of anonymous bumps, but a few yards beyond, where the highway curves past the old Jesus Saves church and you can see Gothics at its (their?) most jagged, cutting into the blue sky some fifty miles distant, or back even further, south of Sabael, where the side road shoots down to the lake and Algonquin, Colden, Marcy, and a fistful of other peaks suddenly appear, an inducement to take them on.

"I can name them all," she said.

    "But have you climbed them all?"

"Not yet. Soon, though. I could do them in one weekend."

"Barefoot."

"Yup."

"Alone."

"Why should I hike alone? You'd actually let me? Aren't you strong enough? We ought to arm-wrestle and see who is stronger."

It never got completely dark that night on Giant Mountain. They finished the hike in the moonlight. She found a bread crust wedged between two rocks, and they split it, and she said, "Pretend there's butter on it. It will taste better than the crappy bread you deliver."

"Name them."

"All right, that's Noonmark and that's Colvin and that's Nipple Top."

"You've got to be kidding," he said.

"Not everybody has a dirty mind."

The trail is so steep that when I look up I occasionally discover a face staring down at me, peering over the edge of a boulder. "Have you seen a guy in a red T-shirt?" she asks.

"Climbing or descending?"

"Climbing. Did you pass a young guy, college kid?"

"I passed a family about a mile ago. All wearing green."

"He's not in green." Her head disappears as I move, avoiding a deer fly.

When I pull up level with her, she says, "Hi," as if such a greeting would not be appropriate until we were at the same elevation. She's dressed in white. White shorts, white golf shirt, white knee socks. Her hair is black, cut short in back, her cheeks sunburnt, as if by a blowtorch.

"What does he look like, besides the red T-shirt?"

"Khaki shorts, like yours. Boots and socks, like yours. No brains." She smiles, not so desperate, then shakes her head.

"You know what might have happened? He might have passed *you*, hiked 'around' the bump instead of 'over'—you know, back where the trail split? There was a sign with those words on it, hand-carved. One route is shorter than the other, and people get separated."

"Thank you, Mr. Trail Guide." She leans against the rock, wipes her face with a clean white towel. "I'm too tired to chase this guy. If you see him up there, would you tell him?"

"What's his name?"

"Michael. And my name is Jackie."

"Are you going to wait here for him?"

"No more than an hour."

"You won't get thirsty?" I'm about to shrug off my pack and offer her one of my water bottles.

"I have a quart of Gatorade," Jackie says. "Not even opened yet. Partially frozen. I'll be okay."

Now I have a purpose for climbing to the top, a reason to talk to people. *Have you seen a guy named Michael? A guy in a red T-shirt?* When I find Michael,

I will say Jackie's name and he will wonder how I know her.

"I went up in a plane once," Regina said, making her hand fly like the wing of a bird. "With this *guy*. Don't frown! Only a one-day adventure. He was a pilot. Not that old, really, maybe in college, still learning. You can see pieces of an airplane wreck on one of these mountains. Not this mountain. They probably didn't carry out all the bodies. Too difficult. It happened twenty years ago. Germans. Nazis escaping from Germany. A lot of Nazis came to the Adirondacks back then, secretly. They own entire mountains up here, with electric fences around them. Is that fair?"

"You went up in a plane."

"We flew below the level of the mountains, this boy and I. I don't even think it was legal."

"This isn't either."

They watched a meteor shower. All at once the lights of St. Huberts shut off. The sky seemed powdered with stars after the moon disappeared.

"Hang onto me," she said. "I don't want to go to sleep and roll off the edge of the cliff."

"I'll catch you."

Everyone descending the mountain this afternoon carries a walking stick, and not just some dead branch picked up along the trail, but a store-bought polished length of ash or hickory, with a leather loop running through a hole on one end. Sixty bucks, downtown Lake Placid. A young man coaxes a young woman down a steep rock, pointing with his fancy stick. "Put your weight forward, Emily. You're gonna keep hitting your ass the way you're going." I stand and watch for five minutes, as he plots her diagonal humiliation.

"But I'm gonna *fall* if I lean forward."

"No you won't," he says. "I'll catch you."

"I'm not sure I trust you to catch me."

"But I will."

The next party is a rebuke to any able-bodied person who poops out before reaching the top. They're all over sixty, *well* over. One woman is blind, a rope tied to her wrist. "Oh, this is great," she keeps saying. "The air is wonderful." She refers to the smell of balsam trees, the needles underfoot. Every time I grab a branch, which I often do to keep my balance, I smell my fingertips, including the index finger still scarred from the slicing incident at Silver Lake, where the sense of touch never came back.

I still have two full bottles of spring water in my pack, half a bag of peppermint candies, no real pain yet. But I could soon be gathering pain and carrying it. I could be the lamest person on the trail.

"Where are we?" the man in her story asked.

"Feel this," Regina said. She moved his hand over the surveyor's bolt that was stuck in the rock.

He felt the letters and numbers. "This is the top, right?" He was on his knees, acting like a blind man.

"We made it."

"Give me one of those mints."

"Sorry," she said. "I'm all out."

"What do these letters say? I can't read in the dark."

"Cryst O Mint."

"No, the letters in the rock, that I'm touching right now."

"Do not remove under penalty of law."

The summit, elevation 4,673 feet (1,410 meters). Ascent from the highway, 3,050 feet (930 meters). Order of height, twelve. Nothing has changed since Regina hiked it, decades ago. If she really did. I'm sure she wrote a poem.

The guy I'm supposed to be looking for at the summit is lying on the rock, sunning himself, his hand touching the benchmark. That must be his red T-shirt rolled up under his neck, closer to gray than red. He's airing his dirty feet, drying his long yellow hair, which is fanned out on the rock and lightly rippling in the cool breeze.

"Think it'll rain?" he says as he sits up, pulling his knees to his sunken chest.

"Are you with Jackie?"

"Oh yeah. Jackie."

"She asked me to pass a message, but I forgot what it was. Maybe she wanted you to slow down."

"I barely know her." He ties his hair in two places with leather shoelaces he's been wearing around his neck, then flips the ponytail back over his shoulder. "Cold, all of a sudden. Freezing. My heart beats, like, once a minute." He puts on his faded red T-shirt. The white letters say, CONTENTS UNDER EXTREME PRESSURE. And there are many large holes in the shirt, as if the contents have exploded from time to time.

"Probably about sixty degrees," I say. The cool wind feels good on my face, like a nice long drink.

"Where's the drinking fountain?" he asks. "They had a drinking fountain on Whiteface."

"No water up here."

"Yeah, I knew that." He's just figured it out. "How about a beer? I'll pay you."

I'm wondering how much he would pay, but I answer, "Nope. No beer."

"I could write you out an IOU." He produces a candy wrapper from his pocket. "You got a pen?"

"Nope."

"All right, here's the deal. I'll give you money. I know you got water," he says. "I heard it sloshing around in your pack."

Really? "None to spare," I say.

"Please? Just a sip, man, is all I need. Really."

"Nope."

"Just pour a few drops into my hands." He cups his hands. The fingernails are long, a quarter inch beyond the fingertips, surprisingly clean. "Please?"

"Sorry." I back away, already beginning my descent. I take a picture of the trail junction sign.

"Have a nice life," he calls out.

"You, too."

"Right." He lies down again. "This is a story for you to tell. I'm gonna *die* up here. If Jackie wants to know where I am, you tell her I died on top of Gigantic Mountain."

"I can do that."

"You could do a lot more!"

Even in broad daylight, downhill is much harder than uphill. I have to sit on a rock to get down from it, grab every tree to keep from tumbling. I hit my ass a couple times, hard, on the rock. Every second I'm unprotected by shade, the sun cooks me another degree. My lips have cracked. I take out one bottle of water and pour it over the top of my head, all of it, with my hat on. Terrific. I never see Jackie again, although I catch up with the party of old people and talk with them a minute (the blind woman worships the sun), and then the family in green, who ask whether they should keep climbing and I tell them they'd better have plenty of water, and they say they have gallons of it. "There's a guy up on top who will buy your surplus."

"Oh yeah?" the father says. "What's he look like?"

"Kid with a yellow ponytail, red T-shirt. Name is Michael. Thinks he's gonna die up there."

"We'll help him if we see him."

"He's a whiner. I'm sure he'll live without your help."

"No," the man says. "We will help him. People have died on nicer days, on smaller mountains."

"He's young and strong."

"He hiked alone? He really shouldn't have hiked alone. So many things can go wrong in the wilderness."

No one ever died of thirst on this mountain. Have they died of anything? Someone could have fallen and died, but I haven't researched the history. This isn't T Lake Falls, where hikers were falling and dying every five years until DEC closed the trail north of the lean-to, the place where the drop-off to the falls came as a surprise after so much level walking, where the rock kept curving more steeply until you could not keep your grip and falling back on your ass might have been the safest thing to do.

Or going barefoot—like Regina. Regina was unprepared and reckless, but her use of the mountains had a kind of dignity. If she ran out of water or went flying off a cliff, in the dark without a flashlight, then she expected to be saved by prayer, if by nothing else. Where is she now? She must be my age, and that is old!

Her note at the trailhead: "We're out. We're done. It must be after midnight."

My note, decades later: "Good hike. Wish I'd had company."

Adirondack Tenors

The drive down to Clifton Park would have taken two hours each way even without the stops in Riparius and Horicon—where Brad would pick up the two other tenors. All three had arrived separately at the first rehearsal of the season. They were new members of the Adirondack Chorale, one of several community choruses in the region. At that time the three tenors knew of each other only by reputation, if at all. Brad was a music teacher for three adjoining school districts north of North Creek, K–12; Albert was retired and living off the grid near Riparius, where he had directed a summer opera festival that had gone out of business after running out of grant money; Luke was the youngest of the three, age twenty-two, living with his parents before heading off to grad school in Michigan.

At the first rehearsal, all fifty singers stood up, one by one, and introduced themselves, including their profession and place of residence, mostly Saratoga County and towns across the Mohawk River. Mostly retired. Later, Brad had said to Albert, standing right next to him, "I didn't know you without the beard,"

142

to which Albert replied, "I didn't know you *with* the beard." Early in the century, they had sat together on a community arts board in Warren County, had argued about something trivial.

Luke, beardless and long-haired, merely grinned and said, "My uncle dropped me off. I need a ride back."

"Three tenors from the Adirondacks," Sylvia, the artistic director said, in front of everybody. She struck a C-major chord on the piano. "It kind of justifies our name."

Adirondack Bank, Adirondack Soda, Adirondack Imaging—none of them actually in the Adirondacks.

"I have a camp in the Adirondacks," a soprano said.

"Me too," an alto added.

"I was actually born there," Luke said, proudly, in his high tenor voice.

"No hospitals anywhere near your town," Albert said.

"It wasn't a hospital," Luke said. "Midwife, my dad helping."

The following Monday, part 2 of the *Messiah* would be the focus. "I'm counting on all you wonderful singers to do your homework," Sylvia said. "You need to visit our website every day. Those part 2 choruses can be tricky."

As the three Adirondack tenors were putting on their coats after rehearsal, Albert said, "I could abandon my 1990 Ford right here in this church parking lot, right?"

"You don't need it up north?" Brad said.

"I don't see any rust," Luke said, leaning over to inspect the vehicle.

"Because it's dark out," Brad said.

"How much do you want for it?" Luke asked.

"Nothing," Albert said. "Deed's in the glove box."

"You sure?" The offer seemed ridiculous.

"I'll sign it over right now." And he did. Of course, it was a *title*, not a deed. Many boxes had to be moved from Albert's car into Brad's car. Blankets, clothing. It took a while.

Sylvia stood by the church door, watching.

"My Adirondack tenors," was all she said.

Heading north, they followed Luke closely until the young man was safely in his parents' driveway, at which point they had a brief discussion, where it was decided that they would carpool in Brad's car, the three of them, to all future rehearsals. "This heap's good for local errands only," Albert said to Luke, patting the old Ford that Luke now owned. "The drive to Clifton Park, don't bet your life on it."

Luke's mother gave him a concerned look.

Brad's elderly passenger was frequently at a loss for words. At one point during the drive north, Albert couldn't come up with the name of his late wife, who had enjoyed a middling career as an operatic contralto. He said he would have to dig up an old concert program to find her name. Had she lived, she might have joined them in the tenor section at Adirondack Chorale. "If you don't mind a lady tenor."

"What are you saying?" Brad asked.

"I'm saying she ended up as a tenor, around the time she hit her sixties. Actually, more comfortable as a baritone. A very good baritone, I must say."

"She smoked a lot?"

"She hid it from me, but I could smell it on her clothes," Albert said. "She'd go out the back door and walk in the woods, smoking. She could have set the whole park on fire. Louise! I remember her name! I haven't *completely* lost my mind. The mention of smoking must have triggered the memory. Louise was her given name. She had several different surnames, for theatrical purposes."

"Shoot one at me."

"You've got me again, buddy. I'll grab an old program tonight and let you know when we ride down next Monday." He sighed deeply, perhaps mournfully. "The cabin is kind of a mess."

"It doesn't matter," Brad said.

"In her day, Louise was fantastic. Like Yma Sumac, who had a four-octave range, by the way."

"Better than that, I would hope. Yma Sumac was a Peruvian freak."

"True. I didn't mean to denigrate my late wife."

Brad was thinking of his own former wife, who was probably still living, and could not sing. Tone-deaf. Hated classical music, covered her ears when he sang. The North Country isolation had driven her crazy. Albert hadn't gotten around to asking about her. Perhaps the subject would never come up, although they would have a lot of miles to fill with conversation before the December concert.

"You know," Brad said, "that kid is moving all the way out to Ann Arbor to study opera. What do you think?"

"Couldn't really hear him, since he was standing in front of us, and not really making much noise."

"Afraid to commit, like many young musicians I've known."

"What was his name again?" Albert asked.

"Luke Schmidt. Not sure of the spelling."

"Oh yeah, right, that's why he looked familiar, minus the hair." Albert coughed violently before continuing. "My wife and I used to conduct workshops for the locals, and he stood out among all the kids. Voice hadn't changed yet. He had a pure high soprano, and nowhere to show it off. A crime, really, for his parents to live so far from civilization."

"Not quite off the grid."

"I guess that's how they put it, Bruce."

"Brad."

"And you can't call me Al," Albert said. "Once is fine, forgiven with a smile. Twice, you're in trouble;

three times, you're dead." He poked Brad on the right shoulder.

"Okay, I'll be careful when addressing you, Albert. By the way, 'You can't call me Al' is actually a variation on the Paul Simon song: 'You *Can* Call Me Al.' My emphasis. No comma, which would change the meaning significantly."

"Who's Paul Simon?"

Luke used Albert's old Ford to haul firewood, jugs of bottled water, groceries, other backcountry necessities. The tires were almost bald; eventually he'd have to get a new set. More likely, retreads. The car might not be registered, might not be insured. His mother's car was dead. Luke would drive her to various part-time jobs—cashier in North Creek, cleaning lady in a motel outside town, nursing home aide.

His mother had homeschooled him, taught him how to read music out of an old Methodist hymnal (PROPERTY OF CHESTERTOWN M. E CHURCH). His father hadn't done much of anything since a hunting accident left him paralyzed from the neck down and unable to speak clearly. Luke's mother and father had met back in the nineties, both attending college in Albany—not music majors, but active in college and community choirs. Nothing existed, no tapes, to show whether Luke's father sang well. His mother had a beautiful voice.

After being homeschooled all the way through his senior year, Luke had gone up to Potsdam to study music. It was the first time he'd ever sung in a choir, which required an adjustment, vocally and socially. He sang in the local Episcopal church, set on an island in the middle of the Raquette River. It was in that church choir that Luke had found his tenor voice, the ease with which he could sing the highest notes. He'd even been assigned the tenor solos in an abbreviated version of the *Messiah*. The choir director there had written the recommendation letter that got Luke into grad school. She had also done the piano accompaniment for his audition tape.

Luke enjoyed the Monday rides down to Clifton Park, listening to the two older men complain about the tenor section of Adirondack Chorale. Like, that guy is way off, and that woman can't hit any high notes. Another tenor had disappeared "from the face of the Earth." Luke wondered what they thought of *him*. Brad had told Luke a week ago, on the ride home from Clifton Park, "You should sing louder."

"But what if I make a mistake?" Luke had said. "What if I hit a bad note?"

"Tenors are always forgiven."

"Why?"

"Because they are tenors."

Albert felt lucky the group didn't require auditions. From the evidence in the soprano section, the lack of auditions had had a negative effect. And the worst voices sang the loudest. They swooped up to the high notes, or as close as they could get. They faded on their way down. For them, "close" was good enough, within a half tone. Their diction was awful, no unison on the vowels. They evidently believed they had wonderful voices, always complimenting each other, hugging each other.

Albert was seventy-five, and some of the ladies were even older. They had to be. An alto said she'd hadn't missed a rehearsal in sixty years! He was not impressed, although he congratulated her and tried to sound sincere. "You can't possibly be that old," he told her.

This was during rehearsal break. He told the alto that he lived off-grid in the Adirondacks in a log cabin and would likely die there.

"Oh dear," she said. "You don't have the internet?"

"I don't want the internet."

"But Sylvia posts recordings there for us to study."

"That's nice," he said. "But I don't need it. You've sung the *Messiah* how many times?"

"Fifty, I think. But, because I can't read music, I force myself to listen to those recordings, or I might make a mistake." She looked over her shoulder. "Sylvia is so demanding."

He didn't tell her he'd never sung the entire *Messiah*, just the familiar choruses, "For Unto Us" and "Glory to God" and the one he refused to name. He didn't tell her he disliked most of it, and he was singing in this group only because his psychiatrist down in Glens Falls had told him to get out of his log cabin and socialize with other musicians—which, in his mind, did not include the banjo-strumming locals who sang in bars and were always getting stories written about them in the *Post-Star*. Brad, although somewhat local, was not typical. He had a trained voice. Actually, he hit all the high notes accurately if not beautifully. And he never missed an entrance, even in the tricky part 2 choruses.

As the time grew nearer to the December concert, they would use the ride to Clifton Park for warming up their voices. Brad, as an active music teacher, took the lead. "Don't be afraid to sound ugly," he told his two passengers. "Scream your heads off," the same advice he gave his combined high school choir—a dozen girls and four boys. The combined band, about the same size and unbalanced in favor of trombones, were told to warm up in private so he wouldn't hear their ugly blasts.

He would drive more than a hundred miles every school day, serving all three districts, and was paid by the mile. They had plenty of money, generated by taxes on lakefront property. The well-paid principals were quite fond of Brad; the woman in charge at Mountain Lake—Dr. Emma Smith—had more than once asked him to join her for coffee at the Mountain Lake Diner. It didn't matter to them that they were now considered an "item" by the locals.

"I worry about you," she said, after a long sip. "It would be nice if you could live right here in town and not have to drive so far every day."

"I'm good."

"You always say that, but don't you ever think, hey, I might just skip a rehearsal down there? And feel all warm and cozy up here in Mountain Lake?"

"Maybe," he said, "but there are two other Adirondack tenors who need to ride with me."

"Oh, you and your tenors," she said. "You and my ex-husband! Wherever he lives now, I'm sure he's lording it over the tenors in whatever group he might be singing."

"That's how we are," Brad said. "That's how we are."

All three had passed the required Covid tests and emailed the results to Sylvia. Actually, Brad had driven to Albert's cabin, ignored the mess in the kitchen, the garbage bags piled up in the living room, the "off-limits" bathroom. He had taken a photo of the definitive red line and emailed it for Albert. "See you soon," Brad had added below the photos. And then, "God willing."

But God was not willing. The Monday before the concert, an ice storm coated the highways in upstate New York, and travel was not advised, especially north of the Mohawk River. Brad ignored the advisory. He defied it. After all, chorale rehearsal had not been cancelled. He had taken his hands off the wheel, just for a minute, to "conduct" his passengers in the obscure *Messiah* chorus, "Let Us Break Their Bonds." He should have kept his hands on the wheel and waited at least until they reached the Northway.

It was the black ice, Route 9, on a curve just north of Warrensburg, with a sign Brad had always laughed at, a sign warning of treacherous driving conditions.

"I want to thank all of you," Sylvia said, "all of you simply wonderful people who came forward with generous contributions to our Three Tenors Scholarship. We now have more than twenty thousand dollars, and we've only just gotten started." The group applauded. The scholarship was in memory of two tenors—Brad Carwell and Albert Fiorini—and in honor of the one survivor, Luke Schmidt, still in Glens Falls Hospital, not quite ready for rehab, whose future as a tenor was now on hold and perhaps in jeopardy.

"I visited him in the hospital," Sylvia said. "They had to shave his head."

Several women gasped.

"His mother was there, singing to him. Beautiful voice."

"Could he even hear her?"

"Oh yes," Sylvia said. "He sang with her."

This was early February, two months after the fatal accident up north. The December concert had been cancelled; the three tenors had been irreplaceable on such short notice. No ringers had been available. The scholarship might pay, long-term, for three new tenors.

"By December, I'm hoping," Sylvia said.

At that very moment, as if on cue, a young man entered the church sanctuary, looking lost. "I'm sorry I'm late," he said. "It was a long drive, and the parking was difficult. I had to throw my coat on the floor."

"Are you a tenor?" Sylvia asked, almost as a joke.

"I might be. I just started voice lessons."

"Where do you live?" a soprano asked. "In the Adirondacks, I hope?"

"It's funny," he said, "but you all know what I mean by the Blue Line, right?"

A couple of men said yes.

"The Blue Line actually runs straight through the middle of our house. It's wild!"

Sylvia knew what he meant. She laughed and said, "So, depending on whether you're eating or sleeping, you might be an Adirondack tenor."

"You got that right," he said. "My dad, too."

Following an extended laugh, a recuperative laugh for sure, they got down to business, with renewed hopes. Anything could happen. The new tenor's father might show up. The next person to enter the church sanctuary might be yet another tenor, a capable one, regardless of whether he lived inside or outside the Adirondack Park.

Untethered

Joan had grabbed her binoculars and driven up from the city. She parked at the Point, where she kept her rowboat and had access rights; actually, she had kept the little boat on dry land, four feet higher than lake level, tethered to a tree, just in case. The specific hour of counting, the "window," was from 8:00 to 9:00 in the morning, and she had arrived at 7:30, untied her little boat, and launched it toward the bay that was her responsibility.

By 7:45 she had counted four loons—two adults and two chicks. She would tell Elise that the observation had occurred at 8:15.

Two years later, Loon Census Day had crept up on her. She was late. The parking area in front of the store was full, as if a huge contingent of loon people had already set out to cover the lake. The loons might be double counted. She bought a coffee and an iced lemon scone, then drove from the store to the Point, got out of her car, and stepped around potholes to the spot where she expected to find her rowboat still tied to the dwarf pine. Of course, it was gone. The space where the boat should have been was now overgrown with purple and white wildflowers, in which random newspaper pages were tangled—from the previous year, somehow surviving rain and snow. Or perhaps the paper trash had blown in recently, on a long migration toward an uncertain fate. The dates and headlines were bleached out, the puzzles unreadable.

Joan felt untethered, in time and space. *That was the word.* It had come up in an old crossword puzzle, not as the clue, but as the answer. She felt as if a stranger had come along and found her tied to a tree, perhaps too loosely, and let her go, let her drift away. Was that a good thing? Not yet, maybe later. She glanced at the lake, as if to spot a loon and count it. Nothing, not even a goose. Elise would know she was lying if she claimed to have seen a loon.

Joan set down her coffee and scone on a flat rock. She picked a wildflower, then dropped it. After a few minutes of lake-gazing—nibbling and sipping—she got in her car and drove to the store, where the loon counters would traditionally gather; and there they seemed to be, but not for long. They were shouting good-byes to each other and taking off.

Like a big family, at the end of a reunion.

It was over. Joan entered the store, tentatively, perhaps for the last time. The Saturday papers were set out, the reserves stacked on the usual metal stool behind the register. The newspaper on top had STEVE written on it in green ink. So many new people!

"I'm confused," she told the clerk.

"About what? We haven't seen you in a while. Did you want to start up your charge book this year?"

"The first thing I'm confused about," Joan said, "is the little rowboat I keep at the Point, where I pay for access. In the off-season, I always pull it up and tie it to the tree. I'm very careful about my routine."

"Yes?"

"The boat is gone. The *tree* is gone!"

"I can't help you there," the clerk said, then turned to a man in a Yankees ball cap standing next to the beer cooler, who might have been eavesdropping. "Max, can you help Janet with her rowboat, the one she keeps at the Point?"

"It's Joan," Joan said.

"No problem." This young man in a Yankees ball cap, whom she might have met a few times before, seemed to know a lot about her, especially her boats. At one point Joan had owned a pontoon boat, a rowboat, and a canoe. Was she now boatless? Max knew she had sold her camp and bought property off the lake, sold her pontoon boat and canoe—actually, Max had negotiated the sales, taken a commission. He talked about all that. But the rowboat was a different story, and he told it enthusiastically, like an over-the-top weatherman—too many hand gestures. He almost knocked a bag of chips off the shelf.

A hand-lettered sign read, IF YOU BREAK IT, YOU'VE BOUGHT IT.

The previous August, the rain had come down gently at first, and Max had been happy about it, because the lake level was low, but then it began to pour steadily, five inches in one afternoon. The wind was powerful—he stood as if leaning into it, smiling—and he saw several boats floating loose, well beyond the docks, a situation he couldn't do anything about—*sorry, ma'am, too dangerous*—so he drove home in his pickup. He came back the next day in his utility boat to discover that several boats, including Joan's, had broken free.

"Why are you smiling?" Joan asked.

"Sorry," he said, and continued his story, still smiling. In the case of Joan's rowboat, the storm must have pulled up the tree the boat had been tied to.

"Isn't that obvious?" Joan said.

Max had scouted the lake for runaway boats, and had retrieved a half dozen, but not Joan's. Someone else might have taken it. He had admired her boat, he said.

"Admired it?" she said. "I don't think so."

Greatly admired it, he continued. Then he told her that a new shipment of sturdy rowboats, fishing boats, had just come in. They were beautiful. Mercury motors, too. Also beautiful.

Joan stared at him. "You're trying to sell me something and I'm not buying."

"I'm just telling you what happened," Max said.

She felt her neck, the place here the knife had almost drawn blood. The gesture had become a nervous tic. There could have been a scar, among her many scars. There was an itch.

In that moment, she decided she was finished with Silver Lake.

Finished with the boats, the loons, the bad weather, the weird locals, the artists and writers. The psychopaths. They were all too much for her. And she said so, in front of everybody. They might never see her again.

On her way out, she stared at the pile of reserved papers. An old joke occurred to her, regarding crossword puzzles. Years ago, she had been sitting across from Emma at the red picnic table, sipping coffee and doing the *Gazette* puzzle and talking as she solved it—to be sociable. She had said to Emma, "Oslo is the capital of Norway."

"So?"

"It shows up all the time. Here's a fact. You might not know that they changed the name of the capital so it would show up frequently in crossword puzzles."

"That's ridiculous," Emma said.

"Used to be Christiania. They changed it to Oslo in 1924. 'Capital city on a fjord' is the usual clue. Of course it could have been. . . . Juneau."

"No, I don't know," Emma said.

They had kept going in that manner until Joan finished the puzzle.

She had overslept that rainy summer day, the year her rowboat had come loose and disappeared. She was in the city. The rain had kept her asleep, added to the soft New Age music of Soundscapes, channel 1943 on her downstairs TV. "Liquid Mind." She always left it on, just loud enough to cover the sound of raindrops hitting the cover of her air conditioner. The rain poured off her roof and splashed on her driveway. In her dream—she was certain it was in a dream, not reality—she went downstairs and out the front door and walked in the pouring rain, still hearing the music. It wasn't that bad. The street had flooded, several inches deep, but she was barefoot, and the water was warm.

Vanishing Point

"Neon red," Steve said.

"What?" Martha stepped on the brakes and pulled over on a wide gravel driveway.

Late summer of 2017, they were driving north on the main highway, well under the speed limit, a mile east of their camp on Silver Lake. They'd been away three weeks, attending weddings and dealing with a large inheritance. Seeing a marriage counselor, as if their marriage might be saved.

They had missed the loon count.

"Who owns this place?" Martha asked. "It looks different."

The property where they had parked used to be a mess—a half-burnt two-story house, plus outbuildings. The house and outbuildings were gone, replaced by a bright red garage and a weed-free driveway. The garage was barn-like, but the color seemed much brighter than barn red. The siding might have been vinyl; the silver-gray gambrel roof might have been fake slate, also vinyl, with a couple of solar panels on the southern side.

"Neon red," Steve repeated.

"Not very Adirondack," Martha said.

"Whatever that is," Steve replied.

His wife may have rolled her eyes at his remark. He wasn't looking at her; he wasn't listening to her description of a museum exhibit in which the proper Adirondack paint colors were displayed. He was staring at the odometer. The numbers didn't add up. Of course, it was her car, so it was entirely her business where she might have driven lately. *Dark brown, faded yellow, deep green, no pink, no blue, no black, nothing too shiny.*

In contrast to the neon red, the double garage door was painted a green so deep that it may as well have been black, with an arched window in the gable above, green-framed, perhaps merely decorative. The building appeared to be uninhabited.

But the house previously occupying that space had been a different matter—overinhabited. The Shink family had lived there, people with dead cars up on blocks, uncountable scruffy dogs wandering loose, uncountable scruffy children doing the same; people who shoplifted cigarettes and beer at the Silver Lake store. A cigarette fire had wrecked the house. The ruins remained standing for years, as if the town could not enforce a final demolition.

Things had changed in Silver Lake over the past decade. There was an art show twice each summer, a historical museum featured in *Adirondack Life*, a "curated"

nature trail, with explanatory signs every hundred yards, most of which had nothing to do with nature, but more about an "oppressive history." *Really?* Steve thought. In the southern Adirondacks?

There was a weekly writing group, mostly poets. There was music. Good music. Lately, for example, a solo violinist had been playing on the opposite shore of the lake, a mile southwest of Martha and Steve's camp. The sound carried over the water, undiminished, even amplified. People claimed to know the identity of the musician, a long-haired kid who had dropped out of Potsdam. So went the rumor. There were no objections to his playing; it wasn't as if some untrained idiot was blaring incompetently on a trombone, or strumming bad chords on an electric guitar turned up to the max. The violin music was actually fiddle music, but quite refined.

"Worth something," Steve said.

"Five cents," Martha said.

"At least."

There should have been a violin case lying open on the musician's dock, to collect donations from boaters, or, absurdly, from swimmers residing in nearby camps. The musician might have been desperate—no college degree, no real job, no haircut. He should have stood at the end of his dock, performing in plain view. If he *had* a dock. He was heard, but never seen.

"It's a recording," Martha said, gazing out the arched front window of their camp.

"No power on that side of the lake," Steve said. "Anywhere beyond Point Vanishing is off the grid. You never see lights after dark. The occasional campfire." Point Vanishing was Steve's nickname for an unnamed bump on the south shore, beyond which the view tended to get fuzzy. Martha preferred Vanishing Point.

"Very faint sometimes," she said, "like a campfire, very romantic."

"Or a musician sitting in a boat, playing."

"Or how about a battery-powered radio?" she said. "A boom box? Some guy sitting on a bed of pine needles in front of his boom box, pretending to play a violin?"

"Don't spoil my illusions."

That had been the theme of that summer. Steve's illusions, challenged if not spoiled by Martha's comebacks. And the fight over the Sunday paper. The fight over *all* the newspapers: she wanted to recycle them and he wanted to use them as fire starter. Especially, the fight when he burned the magazine section of the *Times* (he'd done the crosswords and the Double-Crostic) before she had a chance to read "The Ethicist" column. *He* had read it before throwing it in the fire. The title of the column: "Was I Wrong to Reveal That My Novel Was Inspired by an Adulterous Friend?" The ethicist didn't think so. Did Martha really need to read that column? For Steve, it was a little too close to home.

The next morning, they walked off their differences, or pretended to. They walked as far as the neon red garage—to take a second look—and discovered an unattached flatbed trailer occupying the parking area in front, dozens of folding chairs stacked and belted down on it. A few hours later, when they drove by on their way to the post office, the trailer was gone.

"The chairs could be inside the garage now," Martha said.

"We're not going to stop and peek in the window." Now *he* was the "ethicist."

"How could we? There's no window on the first floor. We'd have to get a ladder to look in the gable window. Do you see a ladder?"

"Check out the porta potty," Steve said.

"No thank you."

At the Lost River post office, while Steve went in to collect their mail, Martha gazed at the adjacent acreage, which was for sale.

"We're not buying that," Steve said, approaching her with a paper bag full of mail.

"You think I want to buy everything. I'm just curious."

It was the old ballfield, overgrown and littered with auto parts, nothing to be curious about.

They picked up the *Times* at the store. Their papers were piled on a chair, three weeks' worth. "Name?"

asked the store lady. She should have known their name. Martha said, "Simson, no *P*," then asked about the red garage while Steve browsed at the beer cooler.

"Shinks's place," the store lady said. "Used to be."

"They've been gone a while," Steve said, setting down a four-pack of Moose Island Ale on the counter, next to the papers. "Right?"

"And they never settled up their bill. Eight hundred dollars!" She gestured at a row of small receipt-type books under the cigarette rack, a couple dozen, each in its own wooden slot, sticking up crookedly. She gestured again, as if to imply that the Shink account book was still there, accruing interest.

"So, I would assume," Steve said, "there's a new owner, whoever put up the shiny new garage?" He handed three twenties and a five to the clerk, who handed him back three pennies.

"If that's what you call it," she said. "You never know what criminal evidence people are trying to hide in their so-called *garage*. The property could still belong to the Shinks, one of Harold's kids who somehow came into money. Drug dealers. I've seen them around. They drive by the store but never come in. I know their cars."

"Not surprised," Martha said.

"You folks want to keep reserving your Sunday paper after Labor Day? My dad drives all the way to Herkimer for the bundle. It's dark at 5:30 in the morning when he gets in the car and tells me he might never see me again."

"Yes," Martha answered, "we'll reserve the paper through the end of September, but not if we're the only ones. Not if it's too much trouble." The ethicist, willing to sacrifice "The Ethicist."

"You won't be the only ones," the clerk said. "Half a dozen new families on the lake asked me to save them a copy. Dad will be driving through the snow every Sunday, just to make them happy."

"Snow?" Steve asked.

"You heard me," she said. "Snow in September."

It wasn't only the thought of an old man driving through snow that bothered Steve. It was the thought of being stuck on one of those northern roads in the middle of a blizzard and running out of safe topics for conversation.

The mysterious violin music always concluded at sunset, never abruptly, as if the musician had walked into the woods while playing, the high notes being the last to disintegrate. "Into soft wind and pine needles," Martha said, musing, almost singing, as they stood on their dock, eight feet apart. Martha stood far enough out to jump in the lake. "I still hear it," she said. "I hear it in my dreams. And then it vanishes."

"Vanishing Point," Steve said. "A point in time, when a person vanishes."

She waited a few seconds, then said, "You could interpret it like that."

"I once played a violin in a dream," he said. "Actually, it happened last week. I wore a tux."

"But you never took lessons." She looked away from him. The lake was more enchanting, she had once told him, evidently to get a reaction. She loved the view. "I doubt you've ever touched a violin," she said. "Or worn a tux."

"You have a short memory."

"Oh yeah, right, our *wedding*." Which she said in such a tone as to imply that their wedding, twelve summers ago, had not gone well. "And in your dream. . . ."

"I was great," he said. "You would have been so impressed, if only you could have listened to my concert. Where were you?"

"Very funny." She gave him a quick glance, not enough to acknowledge his humor.

"The sound was real," he continued. "Perfectly in tune. I had memorized all the notes. Like the story about a guy who practiced and practiced and hired his own orchestra and somehow managed to perform the Mendelsohn violin concerto in public."

"Fiction," Martha said. "We read it together for Intro to Lit. Fifteen years ago. Barry Targan."

"We? Together? You turning the pages and me looking over your shoulder?"

"Too cheap to buy your own copy. Me writing the critical essay about it."

"Right," he said. "I owe you."

"I even took an Art History test for you, eight o'clock in the morning. Aced it. And you, you never even played the *piano*. Not even 'Five Easy Pieces.'"

"Jack Nicholson. He faked it, right?"

"And yet, for some reason," she continued, "we've had a piano in every house we owned, with music propped above the keyboard, waiting to be played. Very risky, because a visitor might ask you to play."

"I would tell them I needed more practice."

"To maintain the illusion."

"Right again," he said.

Every house included their three-season camp on Silver Lake. Rustic dark brown siding, knotty pine on the interior walls. Three beds, three baths. Martha thought they should live in a "Great Camp." Steve had a pretty good idea where she had come up with the idea.

Their place on Silver Lake had an upright beige Wurlitzer in the northwest corner of what they called "the music room," which featured a broken banjo on the wall and an authentic Victrola on a side table—it came with the camp—and a wooden box full of slab-like seventy-eights in terrible condition, the best of which was a novelty recording of a long-dead fool trying to play a trumpet accompanied by raucous, old-fashioned laughter. One-hundred-year-old laughter. Steve loved it. Martha didn't. "If you have to play it," she said, "play it when I'm not around."

The opposite shore had begun to vanish in the dark. Steve cleared his throat and said, "One could refer to unplayed pianos as 'piano-shaped objects.' An unplayed piano only looks like a piano. It raises unreasonable expectations."

She countered with, "And an unseen violinist only sounds like a violinist. I want to meet him." She brushed past Steve as she exited the dock.

"The guy across the lake? You'd have to take a boat." Steve continued looking toward the opposite shore, the three lights that had winked on, evenly spaced.

"And you would never row me there."

He said nothing. She was correct. He would not aid and abet.

"Or I could take a very long walk."

"I'd have to go with you."

"Okay." Said very slowly.

But they never took that walk. It would have been a strenuous *hike*, with frequent bushwhacking.

On the store bulletin board were posted dozens of business cards: stump grinding, house jacking, babysitting, boat washing. A professional fishing guide with her own boat. "I like *that*," Martha said, touching the card, lingering for a few seconds. "I would pay for the experience." A new poster featured a photo of the shiny red garage, its door open, the interior inscrutable. The poster advertised a classical concert for the Sunday evening before Labor Day, free admission ("donations welcome"), featuring an unnamed string quartet. Of course, Martha and Steve attended. The garage was only a fifteen-minute walk from their camp, and they brought flashlights in case the concert ran long.

"The poster didn't indicate who or what," Martha said as they walked along Lakeshore Road before turning uphill toward the main highway.

"Does it matter?"

"You might get to meet your mystery violinist from across the lake."

"*Your* mystery violinist," he countered.

"I'm not exclusive. I've heard other violins on my solitary walks. And cellos. The musicians have proliferated."

"That's one way to put it," he said. *Not exclusive.* It seemed as if she was hinting at something, had been hinting all summer, and he had been oblivious. When she asked him one evening about what features he would "amend" (it could have been "emend") if he were to paint her portrait, he laughed and said, "None." Nevertheless, the white streak in her long black hair—though natural—had begun to annoy him.

Twenty-four folding chairs had been set up inside the neon red garage, four rows, six seats in each row, with a narrow aisle down the middle. "An unknown impresario," Martha commented. "Possibly the property owner." The interior walls were whitewashed plywood, the floor was gravel, a continuation of the driveway. An unpainted plywood stage had been installed up front, one foot high, and twelve feet across, deep enough for four musicians' chairs and their music stands. A utilitarian light hung above the stage, possibly solar powered. Ten minutes early, Martha and Steve seated themselves in the back row, leaving an empty chair between them, on which Martha placed her white leather purse. "Tip money," she said. They watched eight or nine additional concertgoers enter the garage, quietly, people they'd seen at the store, at the Town Museum, older couples who nodded at them. Camp owners or renters. A young guy Steve had never seen before, wearing a rustic wooden cross, sat alone in the first row.

A door opened behind the stage, barely wide enough for the fifty-something cellist to squeeze through with her instrument, followed by the thin male violist, who had no problem, and the two male violinists, both bald and overweight, walking sideways. Light applause.

"Some people can play more than one instrument," Martha said.

"You mean, our mystery violinist might be the guy with the viola."

"I'm just saying. Trying to make it interesting for you. Not your usual kind of event."

"And I'm saying, neither of the violinists looks cool enough to be our so-called mystery violinist from Point Vanishing."

"Very true." Then she said, *Vanishing Point.* Must I insist?"

Whereas: the violist had a substantial man bun and looked as if he hadn't shaved for a couple weeks, and was younger, by at least a decade, than the other members of the quartet. All four wore black pants and turtlenecks, the young violist being the only one who looked good in the outfit.

No introductions, no genial host to welcome the tiny audience. The musicians tuned to each other, the first violin nodded to his quartet partners, and they launched into the Ravel, which Martha recognized right away.

"I'll take your word for it," Steve said.

"They're good," Martha whispered. "You could tell without even listening, just from their body language. WMHT should have sent a sound engineer. They like to support local musicians."

"We're a hundred miles from Albany."

"Don't talk so loud," she said. "The cellist is giving you the evil eye."

Steve's mind wandered. Classical music—mostly wordless, or in a language he didn't understand—held no meaning for him, except in dreams. The piece entailed thousands of notes, beyond Steve's comprehension. Were there any wrong or missing notes? He had no idea. He couldn't separate out the instruments, their sound was woven so tightly.

"And then they unraveled," he said, thinking Martha would appreciate the cleverness. Then he said it again, accenting the final syllable, creating a new word. She laughed briefly.

"While you were in the porta potty," Martha said, nodding in that direction, "I talked with the violist." The musicians were getting into an unmarked white van, the other members of the audience dispersing. The last to leave the venue was the rustic cross guy, who offered a half wave as he got into his BMW.

"The man bun."

Martha looked confused. "Oh, you mean the *musician*."

"Who did you think I meant?"

"The violist's name is Colin, and he's not your mystery violinist. He plays only the viola. He said it would be too confusing to play both instruments, which has to do with the fingering, the way the strings are tuned."

"So it was a *viola* that we heard playing across the lake."

"I don't think so," she said. "Colin lives in Saratoga, grew up on Long Island, but no accent. He got rid of the accent, he told me, not that I asked about it. He went to Bard, not Potsdam. He's never visited the Adirondacks before, despite the proximity to Saratoga. In fact, he got lost on the way up and had to ask directions from a scary local—the words he used. Scary local."

"The local could have been a Shink. We should check for any Shinks lurking behind the garage. And the other musicians?"

"Gerald, Patrick, and Elaine. Last names unknown. None of them live on Silver Lake or even near it," she said. "I have no idea who got them together and brought them here. It might have been the owner of this garage. I didn't ask. But they were really good."

"Maybe it was the other man bun. Who got them together."

"Your fly is open," she told him.

"You changed the subject."

"What I said."

On the walk home, Martha kept pointing her flashlight at Steve's face, as if to read his expressions, which varied minute by minute.

"You're blinding me," he said.

"I'm sorry to have spoiled your illusions. I won't do it again."

"You tipped the musicians, I figure."

"I gave each a hundred dollars," she said. "That's all."

Pocket change for Martha. *That's all.* He still thought the violist—Colin—could have been the mystery violinist, and Colin had lied to Martha about being new to the Adirondacks—after all, he lived in Saratoga—and about his inability to play the violin. He could have been a local kid who went away to college and then, jobless, drifted back to Silver Lake. Might have been one of those young locals who posted notices on the store bulletin board, offering to clean camps, haul away trash, drive the elderly to their medical appointments. It wasn't enough. They were poor. They played for free. Steve imagined Colin standing barefoot on the very end of a Silver Lake dock, in

T-shirt and shorts, hair down, playing an Irish bal-
lad, whatever his ethnicity. He could have been Irish,
Scandinavian, Polish, Russian. WASP. He could have
been trespassing. He had no place on the lake, could
not afford even to rent.

Usually such concerts, even the smallest and most
obscure, would have a program offering extensive
details about the performers. Like, "assistant con-
certmaster of the Hudson Valley Philharmonic" or
"part-time conductor of the Glens Falls Symphony."
Bard College? What the hell was that? Martha certainly knew, but he didn't care to ask her. She would
have gone off on an accusatory tangent.

"Look at me," she said.

"It's getting dark," he said. "It's September. You're
vanishing."

"Good one."

The TEXACO sign in front of the store was illuminated by a flickering spotlight.

"The store lady needs to fix that," Steve said.

"I'd love to watch you tell her."

"So I won't."

"But it would be the ethical thing to do," Martha
said.

*The ethical thing to do would be for you to tell me what's
going on, and for me to forgive you. Especially the forgive-
ness.* The other store lights were off, except the green-
and-red Christmas string that stretched along the

eaves year-round, several lights missing or dead. Soft music played, close at hand—fiddle music, an old guy in a white beard and neon orange ball cap perched on the front porch, legs dangling over the edge. In another context, he might have been assumed to be homeless. Martha and Steve stood in the shadows, flashlights pointed down, but the old man saw them, and when he stopped playing, they applauded and walked over to speak with him. They turned off their flashlights. Martha spoke first and asked if he'd ever played his violin along the south shore of the lake.

"Too far," he said. "Too wild. I don't get out much. Daughter keeps me on a short leash. Not literally, ha ha. My legs don't work too good anyway." He vaguely pointed with his bow. "I live upstairs."

"You do the newspaper pickup," Steve said. "Sunday mornings."

"My only job. It keeps me out of trouble for a couple hours a week. The rest of the time, they don't know what to do with me. I'm not allowed to touch the cash register, which is odd, you might think, since I technically own the business. Four generations in the Olmstead family. Of course, I went away for a generation, then returned. All was forgiven." He chuckled, set down his bow, and rubbed his hands together. "Turning cold a bit early this year," he said. "Could snow in a couple weeks."

"We heard," Steve said, with a genuine shiver.

"We enjoyed your playing," Martha said, stepping closer to the old man. "You should play in public."

Maybe she wanted to put him on stage in the neon red garage, set up an event with the unknown owner, introduce the old fiddler to an audience, and tell his heartwarming backstory. Bring in the sound engineers from WMHT or North Country Radio. She would figure out what to do with him. After all, she had recently told Steve she needed a project, to "spend down the inheritance."

Steve said nothing.

"Very Adirondack," Martha continued.

"Thank you," the old man said. "Nobody's ever said those words to me."

As if "very Adirondack" were the highest form of compliment. They kept talking, oblivious to the lights flashing from inside the building, the store owner evidently signaling "bedtime" to her father. Or she didn't care for his music. He retuned the violin and played another song for Martha and Steve, an upbeat one-minute piece he had composed but never written down. "I keep a lot of stuff hidden in here," he said, tapping his forehead with the middle of his bow. "Safer there, if you know what I mean."

"I love it," Martha said. The store lights flashed again.

"You might be the only one," the old man said.

Steve was thinking of a different violinist, much younger and smoother, perhaps imaginary. He might have been imagining himself as he had appeared in his dream, in another note-perfect performance at an un-disclosed location, wearing a tux, perhaps as a member of a quartet. Martha elbowed him and he finally said, "It's really good, sir. I mean it."

"Thank you. And I'm not 'sir,' not by a long shot. You can call me Abraham."

"Abe?" Martha asked.

"Never that. Just Abraham." He set down his instrument and leaned forward with a deep sigh. He coughed and spit into a nearby bush. It turned out that he couldn't read music. "Not one note." His instrument had been "homemade" more than eighty years ago, for his father, by his father's father, both of whom had played "much better than I ever will, but never in public, far as I know. Too late to ask, ha ha." Which became something else to imagine—for Steve and perhaps for Martha—the music of Abraham's grandfather in his prime, the notes wafting over the surface of Silver Lake, perfect, timeless, more real than any music they had heard this past summer.

On their brief walk along the north shore road to their camp, flashlights turned back on, Steve said, "So much for my illusions," expecting a sharp answer from Martha, or a bright accusatory beam in his face, but she kept her flashlight pointed straight ahead, without the slightest quaver to the focused circle of whatever occupied her mind.

Vanishing Point. Point Vanishing, his choice, might have been too place specific. *Vanishing Point* was the name of a painting on display at the Town Museum, unsigned, with no artist's statement. Just the painting, hanging among various amateur works by locals, this super-realistic representation of the wake of a boat—possibly a canoe, possibly neon red—in which the waves in the foreground were wide and soft, and those most distant seemed to be vanishing around a nameless point of land, curved to the extent that the viewer could not tell what kind of boat it was, nor where it was heading.

A Fish in the Piano,
a Piano in the Fish

I rented on the same island twelve summers in a row, hunkered down in a tiny A-frame only three hundred feet from Carinne's log mansion on the Big Island of Silver Lake, her "great camp." I was close enough to hear the inimitable laugh, though not close enough to get the facts straight. In the end, when Carinne was dying, off-island, where her family owned another mansion, it must have been an imposter imitating her laugh. It could have been a man, a bird, a plane. The laugh wasn't all that inimitable, actually, and from a distance, with so many coniferous trees separating the two properties, all drunks sounded the same.

One thing I have learned: just because you make music with a woman—she at the piano; you, nearsighted, leaning over her shoulder and peering over the top of your glasses to squint at the Broadway lyrics—does not mean you know anything about her. It doesn't even give you the right to know. That our behavior might have looked sketchy gave her all the more reason to protect me in my ignorance. *Married woman and single man together in an isolated Adirondack great camp.* They had a piano in the front room, a baby grand brought over by boat, an event worth witnessing.

It happened sixty years ago. Carinne's mother, Elise Woodruff, gave me the details one morning—at the store, while we were waiting for the stragglers to come back from the latest loon count, discussing the history of boats on Silver Lake

In those days there had been a barge operating on the lake, the length and width of a house and completely flat, with a forty-horsepower Evinrude on the back and a two-foot-high fence to keep any cargo from rolling off. Without the fence, a grand piano could easily have rolled off into a watery oblivion. The day had been windy and the waves high, Elise said. Her parents had told her to stay inside, watch from her bedroom window and look away if anything bad started to happen. The piano, covered in canvas, was tied down, and a boy sat on top wearing a wide-brimmed hat. If the piano broke the fence and rolled off the barge, the boy would go with it. One hoped he would act quickly and separate himself from the piano, not sink into the lake—what Elise had worried about, sixty years ago. There had not always been a fence on that barge. It was installed after an accident involving the occupant of a faulty wheelchair during a big storm, during which it would have been wise to wait on the other side—at the municipal dock, three miles away, where the cars were parked and boat tanks could be filled with gasoline.

The occupant of the ill-fated wheelchair had not screamed in terror when the chair rolled off the barge, as if he or she had wished for an unceremonious death at the lake, on the lake, and finally, *in the lake*. This was not the way Elise talked about it, during the months following Carinne's death; merely the way I interpreted it. In any case, her daughter had not *died* in the lake; she had only asked to be *buried* there, her mother explained, keeping the two deaths separate and distinct.

Moving the grand piano from boat to dock and up-hill to the cottage required half a dozen strong men. Elise, then nine years old, had watched from her dormer window, holding a cat with which she was sharing a dish of ice cream. The cat also watched, as the men unhooked the ropes, removed the tarp and flung it to the side, grabbed all the corners. There occurred some bobbling of the piano during the transition from boat to dock, much shouting and laughing. The boy in the wide-brimmed hat fell into the water—which was shallow, marked by a few sharp rocks. Several times that summer, the young Elise had taken one hundred giant steps from shore without getting her chin wet, turning back when she stepped on an object that felt more like bone than rock. A skull! She had kicked it away. The west end of the lake never got deeper than six feet. A person could walk across to the other side, as proven by a seven-foot-tall man, who evidently conducted the same test on many Adirondack lakes and issued a detailed pamphlet about his findings.

When the boy fell into the water, young Elise, watching from the dormer, had nodded, as if a wish had come true. Five minutes later, when the boy reappeared on dry ground not wearing his hat, she believed him to be a different person, as if the original boy had never resurfaced—a thought troubling her for many years. She waited for his hat to wash ashore, even a piece of it. She was too young to read any newspaper reporting the boy's disappearance; and, later, when local history might have provided an account, she avoided the topic. Her own family was a topic—the Woodruffs, who had originally owned a hundred thousand acres of Adirondack forest, and had lived for several generations on the proceeds from selling off various-sized parcels. No one had—or needed—a job.

My relatives on the lake, the Biedermanns, always worked, and sometimes it wasn't enough to live on. Other locals—the Shinks, the LeBeaus, even the Olmsteads—might skip a month or two when it came to paying their bills. I was relatively lucky, having skated so far on scholarships and government grants.

As for the boy who fell in the lake during the long-ago piano delivery, I already knew a version of the story. The boy was my uncle Tom Biedermann—who left Lost River before I was born. Disappeared, presumed dead. The case with several people in our family.

The piano in Carinne's camp had a bruise on the flat side, shaped like a fish. During a break in our rehearsal I touched the bruise, thinking it might be soft, possibly wet.

"What's wrong?" Carinne asked. "What are you doing?"

"You sure this piano hasn't been underwater?" I said. We were rehearsing to perform at a wedding, off-island, a wedding that was eventually canceled.

"Ask my mother," she answered.

Elise was in the city, a hundred miles away. The two women alternated at the island estate, as if by formal agreement. They would fly personal flags from the pole by the dock, indicating who was in residence— mother (red-and-white stripes) or daughter (checkered blue and white). All Carinne would say about the rift between mother and daughter was that Elise hated Carinne's husband.

"When a car has been in a flood," I continued, "and they secretly clean it up before selling it, the buyer might notice something fishy, like a residual smell, or a real fish flopping around in the trunk."

"There's a fish in my piano!" Carinne lifted her fingers from the keyboard, which reminded me of the 1960s commercial where the woman in the nail salon is told she is soaking in Palmolive liquid.

"So to speak," I said.

"What's that supposed to mean?"

"There's a fish in everything, if you think about it." A spontaneous bit of wisdom, of which I felt rather proud. "Could be a lake trout." I gave the piano a light pat. "Hey, fish," I said. "We know you're in there."

"If you say so." Carinne did not smile, her fingers still raised above the keyboard.

"Come on, Carinne, talk to it. The fish is waiting." I had not charmed her. I had no idea what she thought of me.

"The piano sounds okay, doesn't it?" she finally said. "Every time you come over, you find another thing slightly wrong."

"The piano is real and present in the room. Of course, if it disappeared, then I would suggest searching the lake. The piano could be in a fish."

"You're so full of it," she said.

"No, really," I said. "I read about this somewhere."

"You're making it up."

"I wish I could take credit."

"You wish?" She finally laughed.

Nothing came from this playful banter, although she invited me back more than once. Maybe she liked my voice. Maybe she liked the challenge of resisting my humor. The one-minute hike through the woods, on the trail connecting the two properties, had the feel of scandal, not unheard of on this island. There were twice as many footpaths as a decade ago, un-marked and tangled, pricker branches interwoven with suspicious strips of cloth—even a bright red necktie! Adding to the atmosphere of scandal, Carinne would call from her front deck whenever I was late, "Are you lost? Are you lost? Come to my voice. I'll bang on the piano until you find me." Such yelling and banging, heard from the opposite shore (sound travelling so clearly over open water) could have been subject to misinterpretation.

One time I arrived for our rehearsal to find her with another man, an attractive young fellow. Blond ponytail, white Oxford shirt with the sleeves rolled up to the elbows, black Bermuda shorts, open-toe sandals. He sat on the piano bench, playing wonderfully. Not her husband. Not even close. The boat taxi was docked below, my cousin Max idling at the tiller, occasionally racing the engine to signal his readiness to leave. I should have known—an off-islander was on the property. A lover.

The young man played Chopin, a polonaise, a nocturne, perfect. He played from memory. I said something like "wow," and he cut off his playing with a harsh chord and a smirking glance in my direction.

"Excuse me for interrupting," I said.

"All done," the young man said.

"He's the piano tuner, idiot," Carinne said.

"About time," I said. "I nearly mentioned it at our last rehearsal. The pitch dropped so low I had to transpose a full tone as I sang." I needed to shut up. My voice was rough, and I hadn't even started singing. "You remember, Carinne, how confused I was?"

"The tuner comes on July 15th every summer," she said, rubbing a key in the highest octave, the most difficult to keep in tune. It made no sound, as if the tuner had disabled it, as if such an imperfection were the artisan's right. She looked at me again. "You knew that."

A different guy, I thought. *Not this guy.* The regular tuner was much older, bald, lame, always coughing. This young fellow looked like he could run a marathon and bench-press twice his weight. He unrolled his sleeves and buttoned his cuffs, then flexed his fingers, no rings.

"I want you to meet Tristan," Carinne finally said, then mumbled his last name. "Graduated this year from Potsdam. You know, Crane School of Music?"

"I've heard of it."

The young man, Tristan, seemed slightly embarrassed. He had color in his face, a wad of chewing gum tucked into his cheek.

"He tunes all the pianos on the lake, taking over for his grandfather. A summer job, something to do until he finds a teaching position."

The young man bowed. "At your service."

We didn't shake hands. Carinne never said my name.

"How many *are* there?" I asked. "Pianos on the lake."

"I have no idea," the young man said. "They keep leaving notes for me at the store. Every time I go in to buy cigarettes, I find a note from a lake resident saying it's been, like, ten years since the tuner came around."

"What do you charge per visit?"

"It's not that my grandpa didn't try," he said. "He had a hard life. Sometimes he'd row all the way to some remote camp only to find it locked up, and there'd be plywood over the windows and doors, and he'd never get paid for his trouble."

"I have no piano," I said.

"Not a crime," he said. "Some jobs, I just show up unannounced and nobody has a problem with it. Carinne didn't mind."

"I was taking a shower," she said.

He smiled. "She likes to make it look wicked."

The young man might not have shaved for several days, perhaps as long as a month. He was one of those guys with a face so pretty he must have felt he had to grow a beard to defend himself. Or *try* to grow one, a few wisps along the jawline and above the lip. The ponytail, though, was substantial. He might have been working on it since high school. He could cut it off for a job interview, or leave it uncut and use it as an excuse for not being hired.

"The lack of a piano is forgivable," Carinne said. "But a real piano becomes a nice thing to have when the power goes out."

Max tooted the boat taxi horn.

"Anyway, here's my card," Tristan said, handing it to her.

Tristan—what a name!—grabbed his black tool bag and descended the hill to my cousin's outboard taxi, one of several businesses that had grown out of his boat dealership. I watched Tristan leap into the boat, causing not the slightest dip nor ripple, evidently weightless. He spit his gum into his hand and threw it in the lake, then he waved at us, assuming, correctly, that we couldn't take our eyes off him. Carinne rubbed away the condensation on the window, humming the Chopin tune. I waited for the sound of the motor to diminish and blend with the wind. Given the extent of a piano tuner's hearing range, one never knew when it was safe to start talking about him.

Finally, I turned to Carinne and whispered, "Does he sing?"

"Why do you ask? And why are you whispering?"

"His voice made me think he could sing. Tenor, obviously."

"You directing a church choir now?" she asked.

"Of course not. Does he sing?"

"I haven't asked him yet," she said. *Yet?*

"Then I'm safe, right? He's just a piano tuner and visits only once a year and has to rent the boat taxi to get across. Right?"

"Safe from what?"

As if to make an even greater fool of myself, I kept talking. "It's not like he's a mechanic and so many things could go wrong you'd have him over twice a week, or more."

"He's not a mechanic. Max does our boats."

Then I studied Tristan's business card, which said nothing about tuning pianos. Only his last name and the word *musician*, a local phone number and a couple of eighth notes. What good would it do a musician to be so unspecific?

Carinne and I never took out the music, that time. She never said my name. I think she was already dying.

After Carinne died, the piano went silent. Elise kept it in the front room as a "nice piece of furniture." She stacked her mail on it, dirty plates, dirty wine glasses, two or three cushions from her old boat, a piece of driftwood shaped like a whale and polished to a high sheen. A half-dozen photos and paintings of loons. "My obsession," Elise said.

The *Best of Broadway* book remained open on the music stand, where we had left it—to "Almost like Being in Love," from *Brigadoon*. A possible wedding song, especially if any doubt existed concerning the level of commitment. The song's lyrics (sung in the movie by Gene Kelly) expressed a pure, unqualified love, a boundless optimism. But *almost*? Was that close enough? I never learned what went wrong with the off-island wedding; it might have happened without music, or with different music.

Despite Carinne's death, the parties at the great camp continued. The husband (widower) showed up for the last party, an overweight passenger on the boat taxi who walked using a cane. Other island residents arrived in their own boats or on foot, swimming part-way. They walked in front of my cabin, trespassing, shaking their wet heads, arguing about what would happen next. Moored at my dock, their yachts bumped against my dinghy.

"What's up?" I would ask.

"You'll see," they answered.

Elise had been commuting back and forth to the island in a canoe with a seat in the middle for rowing. Her technique was impressive, smooth and rhythmic, as if she'd done this in college. Sometimes the oarlocks squeaked. Sometimes she would bump into her dock and say, "Oh," or drop a grocery bag in the water when unloading and swear mildly and then say to herself, "Just leave it there." On the night of the last party, I saw no canoe along the shore, which seemed odd, since the party was her daughter's funeral. Elise was in the city.

I was not invited to the funeral, but I went. The island wasn't big on formal invitations. If you felt in a mood to party, you grabbed a flashlight and walked toward the noise. Fireworks, tom-toms, people screaming. If it was loud enough, you figured the whole island was invited. If the lights shone bright enough, you found your way without a flashlight. A two-mile path ran the perimeter of the island, sometimes widening into a lawn, often narrowing into a thicket of wet mountain maple and scrub hemlock—abandoned property, struck by lightning and burnt to the foundation and chimney. The state wouldn't maintain the trail, since there was not one square inch of state land on the island. Outsiders—off-islanders—would drop anchor in the deepest part of our bay and turn up the volume on their radios, while they jumped and swam from their anchored boats, as if they belonged here, too.

"Sounds like she wrote down what she wanted, every little detail," Elise said, after I told her what had happened, redacting the most troubling parts.

"The violin boat arrived first," I said.

This was an elongated rowboat, more stable than a guideboat—a violinist at each end with a rower seated in the middle. The water remained calm. The violinists stood and played a Bach two-part invention, a slow dance by Grieg, then a version of Samuel Barber's "Adagio for Strings" arranged for two parts. One violinist was Tristan, the young piano tuner. Black T-shirt, black pants, like an orchestra player on dress-down Thursday nights. Same long blond hair, but hanging loose down his back, blowing away from his face. Clean-shaven. He might have snagged an orchestra job. I could picture him as the rehearsal accompanist for an opera company. Or a sub in the last row of violins.

When I mentioned him, Elise recounted how, years ago, the grandfather would row over to the island and stay too long after tuning the baby grand, as if expecting a meal, a cocktail, or something more, something impossible. "My husband wouldn't be far away, up on the bluff, felling trees." She grimaced. "He didn't like to be in the room while the piano was being tuned."

"I can imagine," I said.

"Back then, the grandfather was just as good-looking as the grandson," she said. "My husband couldn't stand the sight of him. And then, as the grandfather grew older, he would bring the little boy along. His apprentice. 'Does that sound okay to you, Tristan?' he would ask. 'Would you hold this tight for me until I say let go?' The grandfather had a rather loud voice."

"Losing his hearing."

"My daughter, unlike my husband, absolutely adored the grandfather. Her first teacher."

"She loved music."

"One good thing you can say about her."

I described for Elise the pontoon boat carrying a brass band, all in spiffy band uniforms. They never came ashore. Four times they passed in front of the camp, slowly, fifty feet out, as if afraid of running aground. They played the blues. The blues, but joyful. They played in tune. Carinne had many friends who played in tune. I have no idea whether these brass players were friends, or merely musicians for hire. A strange gig—this Viking funeral. Max later told me that some of what happened was "illegal."

Next came the dancers in black leotards, disembarking from a large pontoon boat onto the dock while turning cartwheels, to generous applause and cheering. The dock, sometimes used for yoga lessons and growing tomatoes, was large enough for a brief ballet accompanied by the violinists. A repeat of Barber's "Adagio." Then, elegantly, the dancers glided back onto their boat and off to the next performance.

"Her daughter studied ballet," Elise said.

"She had a daughter?"

"First husband," she said. "He had custody."

"So, one of the dancers was her daughter?"

"How would I know?" she said, remarkably dry-eyed.

I described only the good things, the *celebration of Carinne's life*, a phrase I quoted without using air quotes. I did not describe the bizarre conclusion, how two men dragged the six-foot-long "boat" from under the camp, carried it to the shoreline, and set it in the water—Carinne's idea of a casket. I like to think there was a fish in there with her, a fish that had swallowed a miniature piano, which, itself, contained a miniature fish, but I'm flattering myself that she would have remembered what I had once said to her about a fish being inside everything. So I doubt it. A woman at the party said Carinne had drawn a diagram and given instructions as to how the boat would be launched and set on fire. Like, *let it go a fair distance out into the lake, toward the middle, then light the match, and see what happens, pray it won't rain*. Everyone drank too much.

The boat hadn't been doused with enough gasoline. Rain fell, briefly. The funeral boat had a little motor on the back that sounded like a toy, sputtering every few seconds. The motor and the fire gave out simultaneously, more than a hundred feet from shore. People were laughing, drinking, talking about Carinne, how she would have enjoyed the scene now playing out. Evidently—and I had no sense of this—she liked it when things did not go according to plan, even when the plan was hers. My cousin Max and a couple other locals got into a utility boat carrying a can of gasoline and box of matches, and some long sticks the size of arrows. They might have brought a bow with which to fire the arrows.

Elise believed that her daughter had been cremated discreetly, the ashes scattered in the woods. She could keep on believing.

The following would have been too much for any mother:

The utility boat approached in a wide circle, deferentially, then pulled in close. Cousin Max tipped the gas can above the little death boat and soaked it (definitely illegal), shook the can for the last trickle, then put the boat in reverse for a few yards. The other guys began lighting matches tied to sticks and tossed them at their target. They kept missing, until one arrow caught in a gap in the wood, and the whole thing exploded. The men jumped back. One man landed in the water, then clung to the side of the boat. People on shore laughed. The little death boat seemed to gain energy, the motor starting up again as the flames increased. It ran in tight circles for a minute, then sank into nothing.

Recounting

July 21, 2018, the usual time and place in front of Olmsteads's store: Elise took out her pen and began tabulating. Max knew everybody, except for the young woman whose badge read, SOPHIE. Late thirties? An older woman named Melody sat across from her, possibly Sophie's mother. Max knew her vaguely from dealing with her antique boat, refinishing the wood, storing the boat during the off-season in shrink wrap, servicing the old motor. Like Sophie, Melody was a first-time loon counter, though a longtime Silver Lake resident.

"I see a few familiar faces," Elise said from her wheelchair, at the head of the red picnic table. The wheelchair had a built-in tray and a black-on-white loon flag sticking up on the back, like the American flag a disabled veteran might fly from his wheelchair. For a second or two, Max pictured Elise out on the highway, bravely moving forward in her chair. He tried to erase the image.

"It's been a few years for some of us," she said. "But all is forgiven!"

"I never went anywhere," Max said.

"You sold me a new boat, and it's wonderful."

"I'm glad you like it."

"Where is Martha?" Elise asked.

"She moved to Mud Lake," her ex-husband Steve said. "If she's counting loons up there, it's none of my business. I'm the loon counter now." He pointed his left thumb at his chest. *Okay*, Max thought, *now she's divorced. Interesting. Mud Lake.*

"Which Mud Lake?" Max asked, although he knew.

"Doesn't matter," Steve said.

Elise checked her list. "I'm surprised Wesley didn't show up this morning. The artist who makes such beautiful maps of his lake. I'm calling his mother."

"I'm not," Max said. "Not surprised." It wasn't as if he needed to put a tracking device on Martha. She had existed only as a distant possibility. More distant now.

"And no Cheryl, no James," Elise added.

"Also not surprising."

"Cheryl?" Melody said.

"Enough about the absentees," Elise said. "I should introduce my new caretaker, Tristan, the official loon counter on the big island this year. As you may have noticed, I'm not as agile as I used to be." A young guy stood up and bowed. Light applause.

Max knew him, but not with a shaved head. The formerly long-haired Tristan wore a too-tight loon T-shirt. Elise might have run out of the larger sizes. Several inches of six-pack stomach were visible above Tristan's bathing suit. Caretaker? Possibly a caregiver.

"And, with eternal thanks to Max," Elise continued, "we now have a beautiful new pontoon boat, which makes everything so much easier. No more rowing, obviously."

"You're welcome," Max said. "Long overdue." He wondered what she meant by *we*. Was it the royal we, or was there a May–December thing going on?

"Tristan tuned my piano," Steve said. "He gives lessons."

Tristan nodded.

"And I finally learned where all that beautiful violin music was coming from."

Again, Tristan nodded.

"I have no piano," Doug said, "but Monty's wonderful mother sold me thirty feet of shoreline on Little Silver, and Max here sold me a boat and a motor."

"Old boat, new motor," Max said. "The age of the motor is what really matters."

"Do they even allow motors on that pond?" Steve asked.

"Five horsepower," Max said. "Perfectly legal. It purrs like a kitten."

"And it's a lake, not a pond," Doug said, raising his voice.

"I meant no offense," Steve said.

"None taken," Max said. He kept the peace among his customers.

Robert, the former front-porch guitarist, who had inherited his grandfather's camp on Silver Lake (the grandfather had lived to a hundred), was about to give his count, when an old woman walked by slowly, within twenty feet of the red picnic table. Robert stuttered and struggled to say, "Two adults, no chicks."

"Hello everybody," the old woman said. "I'm back." Then she resumed walking north, into the wilderness, keeping a steady pace, her long white braid bouncing.

"I thought I knew everybody," Max said.

"You're not old enough," Robert said.

"Okay, team, let's focus," Elise said, knocking lightly on the table with her arthritic right hand. "We're tabulating!"

Caretaker or caregiver. With his mother gone, the double-wide sold, Max was no longer a caregiver. He had his own place now, on Narrow Bay. Sixty feet of shoreline, old dock, no beach, the smallest camp on Silver Lake, a fixer-upper with salmon-pink asbestos siding, no insulation. But *on the lake.* The markup on a dozen pontoon boats had covered most of the down payment, plus a $30,000 profit just on Elise's fancy barge, which, with alterations to her dock (and the store dock), was now wheelchair accessible, even when the lake level dropped. Off-season, Max was somewhat of a caretaker for his neighbors. Robert, for example, had said to him, joking, "You never know who might be sitting in your living room when you return after a winter in the city." Like who? The woman with the long white braid?

A total of twenty loons, adults and chicks, had been properly counted on Silver Lake and Little Silver Lake, a record. Mud Lake was unaccounted for.

"Before we go," Robert said, now speaking calmly, "I have something special I'd like to show you all. It's a photo I took the other day, at the museum. *Our* museum, just down the road." He produced a rolled-up sheet, slipped off the rubber band. "I went downtown to have it blown up. I need a couple of rocks so I can spread it out for you." Max found several, placed one on each corner, and the loon counters were able to get a good look at the photo, which measured about two feet by three feet.

"That's exquisite," Melody said.

Robert nodded. "You're looking at a photo of a painting, which is even larger than this and beautifully framed. Our leader, Elise, very kindly donated it to the town museum."

"Wesley who?" Sophie said, staring closely at the artist's signature.

"Actually, he wanted to be anonymous," Robert said. "The title is *The Loon Counters*."

They all leaned in and studied the photo of the painting. It was quite realistic. The red picnic table, somewhat elongated, occupied the foreground. The lake was visible in the background, with a family of loons swimming left to right. Eight people were seated at the red picnic table, four of whose faces were visible.

"Shouldn't they be looking at the lake?" Sophie asked. "*Counting* those loons?"

"That's the whole point," Robert said. "Those four loons may or may not have been counted. The point is that the window is closed, the one hour of counting has passed. They've done their duty, as have all of us today."

"You're not in the picture, Elise," Melody said.

"I asked to be excluded. 'Vanity working on a weak head produces every sort of mischief.' Jane Austen."

"I only recognize one person," Max said. "The guy in the lower left corner of the painting, with the smirk on his face. The artist himself."

"Is he a loon counter?" Sophie asked.

"If he is," Steve said, "he's not sharing."

"All right, everybody," Elise said. "Move the rocks and roll it up, Robert. People can stare at the original for hours, if they want. This wonderful painting now hangs in the Town Museum, on permanent display."

"So the point *is*," Steve said, staring at where the picture had been, basically talking to himself, as the others had grabbed their coffees and left. "The point is that *we weren't there*, it was one of those loon-counting days that existed only in the artist's mind, that existed only for the purpose of turning it into a painting. Case closed."

Baseball in the Adirondacks

August 2019. Max and Robert are neighbors on Narrow Bay, the north shore of Silver Lake. Robert has questions concerning postcards that were part of his grandfather's collection.

"I knew you'd be interested," Robert says, smiling. He has fanned them out on his well-polished dining room table—a couple dozen postcards from the previous century, which include the old Methodist church (now the Town Museum), the fire tower (gone), the ski area base lodge (gone), a beach that used to be public, canoers on Little Silver Lake, a set of snowshoes hanging on an anonymous wall (the message on the back: "Too cold for that"), a young man standing at bat on the Lost River baseball field, with other players vaguely visible in the background.

"Could be my grandfather," Robert says. "Check the postmark. 1935."

"Wow."

"Or the father of my old handyman, Harold Shink, bless his soul. Also named Harold Shink. Made it to the minor leagues, one season at Binghamton. I could go on. Harold Junior talked more than he actually worked, but I forgive him." Robert is now the town historian.

"If he only did one season in the minors," Max says, "he'd have no place in baseball history."

"A shame. Ahh, history." Robert is looking out the window at the lake. "Our athletes are part of town history. Cheryl LeBeau, who made the 1984 Olympic team."

"Yeah," Max says. "She went back to using her maiden name. I'm sure you could tell me what happened. Or keep it a secret."

"And other athletes we've forgotten. I need to do a deep dive into this."

Max is looking for a connection to his own family. "Do you have any more postcards with local baseball players? Maybe from the sixties or seventies?"

"Haven't seen any. Here's a good one—showing the store where you worked."

Max frowns. "Not while I worked there, Robert." The siding is salmon pink. The porch is too small. The gasoline brand above the pumps is wrong.

"If you look really close," Robert says, "you'll notice I'm not sitting on the porch playing my guitar. I haven't been born yet."

Funny. Robert has talked about that era in store history. The guitar still exists, tucked away in Robert's camp. Max wants the postcard with the ballplayers. Wants to own it, frame it, hang it on one of his bare walls. But it has sentimental value for Robert, with its fuzzy shot of the guy Robert thinks is his grandfather, or the father of his late handyman. Or the batter could be Jack Gerling.

Before Max leaves, Robert tells him about a visitor to the Town Museum, where Robert has an office.

"Big fellow, about your age, well-dressed, comes knocking on my door. He's looking for his mother."

"Weird."

"His *birth* mother," Robert says. "DNA and all that. He's looking for Joan DeWitt."

"Long gone," Max finally says.

"I told him about the note she left on the bulletin board at the store."

"Crazy note. Diane took it down, last year I think. You know, I finally found Joan's little boat. Is this guy still around?"

"Didn't even leave his card," Robert says. "Just shook his head and drove away."

"Some people, when they leave the Adirondacks—I mean Joan—they leave no trace."

"Exactly."

The next day, Robert comes over to Max's place to look at the baseball cards Max recently discovered in the downstairs bedroom closet, in a pink shoebox. The old woman from whose estate Max bought the camp must have forgotten the box existed, or assumed there were pink shoes in it. He has already gone through the box looking for Jack Gerling's card. Nothing. That morning, after stopping at the Motor Vehicle office (boat registrations), he visited the county library and used their internet to see whether such a card existed. Several showed up—fifty dollars (fair condition), eighty dollars (good), two hundred dollars (mint). A newcomer to the world of baseball cards, he has no idea whether these are fair prices.

"Okay, let's see what you have," Robert says, seated across the folding table from Max. "I'm no expert." He steadies his thermos. "I'd hate to spill coffee on anything."

"You'd think *I* would be the expert, but I never got into it." Max sips from a Yeti water bottle. Hates coffee. "Baseball cards seemed like a hobby for people who couldn't actually play the game."

"I collect old books."

"Which makes sense," Max says. "You're a writer, a historian. You keep asking me to join your writing group, and I keep putting you off." Robert's camp has an entire room dedicated to reading and writing, with historic maps and author photos on the walls.

"We're losing members," Robert says. "They age out, they disappear."

Max won't commit. "I'm sorry about this rickety table," he says, "but it's the only one in the camp. I haven't gotten around to fixing up the place, except to have the roof repaired."

"Always the top priority," Robert says.

The pink shoebox is stuffed with hundreds of cards. "She must have been a big fan."

"Her son," Robert says, then sips his coffee. "A character. He died ten years ago. Now it's just a bunch of second cousins in California who were happy to sell the place."

"A son? How come I never met him?"

"Very shy. And a hoarder," Robert says. "I helped clear out the camp, two summers ago, before you bought it. Old newspapers and unpaid bills. I've seen worse. Okay, let's take a look at the cards."

They divide them into two piles and agree on a system. They agree that they know enough about baseball to be able to tell the winners from the losers. The losers get thrown on the floor. About halfway through, it's 10 percent winners. Mantle, Robinson, Berra, Maris, Musial, Banks, even a few rookie cards, some vintage cards with vaguely familiar names. Christy Mathewson. Monty Ward. Grover Cleveland Alexander.

"Monty," Max says. "The name rings a bell."

"You're thinking of our Monty. He's long gone."

"Tell me about it."

"You mean, you want the actual story?" Robert closes his eyes, breathes deeply. "Okay, one short paragraph. I've known him since the seventies, when he was just this local kid, seemingly with unlimited potential. I'd be playing my guitar on the store porch, and he'd pull up a chair and sit facing me. If I sang something, he'd try to sing along, but there would be a one-second delay, and weird distortion."

"Crazy even then."

"Actually, not then. But a few years later, his mother had him institutionalized."

"Before that, did he play ball?" Max asks.

"Probably not."

"We should be wearing gloves," Robert says, nervously moving his coffee thermos to the floor. "Do you have internet?"

"Not yet," Max says.

"As I said, I'm no expert, but I've got sixteen cards in my winners pile that I'm eager to research online. We can do it at my place."

"I've got a few in my pile."

No Gerlings.

If the online prices are to be believed, the best cards from Max's bedroom closet add up to more than a million dollars. "I can help you," Robert says. "I'll help you negotiate. You need to beware of the scam artists who are active in the world of sports memorabilia. You might need a lawyer, a safe-deposit box at your bank."

"A bodyguard, right?"

"Right. If you sell the cards for what they're worth, you'll never have to work again."

"I don't mind working."

The two men are standing in Robert's library, where he keeps his desktop computer. They switch back and forth among several so-called legitimate websites.

"We need to talk to the experts," Robert says. "How about a road trip to Cooperstown?"

"Sounds good."

"You could tear down your camp and put up something nicer and still have enough money to live comfortably without ever working again." Just because Robert has never had to work for a living—spending all his time hiking and writing poems—doesn't mean that Max should follow his example.

Max has other ideas. *Baseball in the Adirondacks.* Not simply a display at the Town Museum, but a "field of dreams" like the one in Dyersville, Iowa. The old ballfield property behind the Lost River post office has been for sale since the beginning of the decade, perhaps the beginning of the century. The property consists of fifteen overgrown but level acres, with a hundred feet of ugly frontage on the highway, trash, old tires, a couple of rusted shopping carts from Price Chopper. They want thirty thousand for the property. If the cards are really worth a million, Max could buy the land, clear it, and build a baseball field, with stands, lights for night games, a paved parking lot. He could start up a summer league, the kind where they play by the old rules and wear vintage uniforms. The players would be locals, a few summer people. He has no illusions about a team of historic players emerging from the woods. He's not crazy. It won't bring back Jack Gerling or his brother Don, but that isn't the point.

Summer 2024. There were rough years in between. The cards were worth only about half what they'd hoped. But Silver Lake thrived. People moved north, bought year-round homes. They bought boats. They traded in old pontoons for new pontoons. Max fixed up his camp, got a girlfriend—Sophie, whom he had first met at the loon counting—married her, and now had a twelve-year-old stepson, Keith.

A person named Francis Biedermann had died during the pandemic. Diane saw the obituary and handed it to Max. "One of yours?" The man had died at age ninety-eight, in Schenectady. The clipping said very little, only that the deceased had been a Methodist minister.

"Never heard about him," Max said. "Or of him."

"There's always a good reason," Diane said, and nothing more.

Max cleared the land behind the post office and created a new ballfield, not as fancy as he had dreamed—no stands for spectators, only a small metal building, open on one side, where the spectators and players could escape from the rain. A gravel parking lot, perfectly graded, no low spots. A sign at the entry welcomed all to Jack Gerling Field.

Keith had questions. How fast was your fastball? Why didn't you play in the Majors? Who was Jack Gerling?

Max took him on a tour, beyond Jack Gerling Field—to the sandbank where, many years ago Don

Gerling's leather mitt, even then moldy and useless, had been buried; the local names that had been engraved into the embankment had, of course, long ago washed away. "I don't see anything," Keith said.

Max picked up a ball-size rock and threw it hard into the sandbank. "Did you see that?"

"Almost didn't."

A Phone Call

Elise, it's Greta, I hope I didn't interrupt anything. The last time I called, I may have interrupted a private activity.

Oh, it was just a massage. It was nothing.

So, is *this* a good time?

Yes. I've been sitting in my living room, staring at the water, the waves breaking against the big rock. Accompanied by live background music. It never gets old. Are you up at Mud Lake now?

No. It's too much trouble to get there. We're in Sarasota.

Will I never see you again?

You could fly down here, Elise! Sarasota has a wonderful airport.

Well, if you'd said that to me only a couple months ago, I would have told you it was impossible, what with having to deal with the wheelchair and all.

I sense some good news.

I'm walking again! And dancing!

With whom, may I ask?

Not in public, but I dance with Tristan, part of my therapy, and it worked. One day, as part of our routine, we put on some music he likes, and I stood up and began moving, and the rest is history.

He's how old?

Oh, Greta, do we have to get into that kind of detail?

I know. I tend to ask questions I would be better off not asking. You don't have to go into any details. But I do think I might be interrupting something.

Not at all. He's playing his violin. I bought him a new one, so he's breaking it in.

Whenever I call Wesley, it seems that I'm interrupting something. He might be painting, or an activity I'm not supposed to know about.

Do tell.

Actually, Elise, I called you today because of wonderful news I have to share. I'm going to be a grandmother!

You could knock me over with a feather.

I should have asked you if you were sitting down. Elise, they have a midwife on call. They might have already installed her in one of the cottages, although there are five guest rooms in the main lodge. The baby could have already arrived.

I'm a grandmother myself. Come to think of it, I might even be a great-grandmother.

I call Wesley once a week. It used to be every day, until Don told me to give it a rest. I was so worried about my son, my only child. In fact, Wesley didn't call *me*. He never calls me. And this latest phone call, I guess he figured he had to let me know they were going to have a baby, and he wasn't sure how I would react, as if I didn't think Martha was the most beautiful woman in the world. She's forty, you know. Maybe older.

We don't do the loon-count gathering anymore—it stopped during the pandemic—so I wasn't aware of what was going on up there. Are they married?

I don't know, Elise. I thought *you* might know.

I'm out of the loop. But I'm glad to hear we're going to have another baby in town. Max and his wife are expecting.

Who's that?

My boat man. Every two years, I do an upgrade and Max finds me the best.

Very good. Up at Mud Lake, we've always had the same boat. Even before I was born, in fact.

The motor must have been replaced by now, at some point, I would assume.

No motor. It's a *rowboat*.

Lovely. You can put a little battery-powered troller on the stern. Max sells them.

You know, Elise, I have to tell you—that very rowboat saved my marriage.

Do tell.

Long ago, even before Wesley was born—which was a miracle—we were having our problems, Don and I. I don't need to get into the gritty details, I've actually forgotten most of them, but the boat was there when

I needed it, securely tied to the dock, ready to launch. So I would say to Don, "I'll be back in an hour," and set off in the rowboat. It's a small lake, you know.

Yes. And very private. Just one other camp.

Hippies. In those early years, I became an expert rower. There were many times when I had to get out of that camp before I went crazy, and I would go and sit in our chapel instead of rowing, and I would even pray for a while—it's a wonderful spot for praying—but more often, I would simply sit and watch the chipmunks skittering down the aisle of our chapel, so carefree. Rowing the boat was more complicated, of course. And I think the complications were good for me. Untying the rope. Centering the cushion. Centering *myself.* Carefully inserting each oar. Pushing away gently, quietly. Focusing on a tree on the other side of the lake, which of course was impractical, a pain in the neck, literally, because, in a rowboat, you're supposed to face away from your destination, though I didn't really have a destination, except to return to the dock when I felt ready, and I would often think about not returning to the dock, but pulling up at the tiny beach on the opposite shore, and walking away.

Leaving Adirondack Park

When leaving the Adirondack Park, you may not be aware of the exact moment of transition. You have passed the park-shaped brown sign without noticing, and now you see, briefly, a beautiful lake, downhill a few hundred yards, a lake set in the "ordinary world" beyond the boundary, an idyllic sheet of turquoise, with a person in a wide-brimmed hat rowing a boat from left to right exactly as you should be doing—instead of leaving—and then the road curves again and suddenly you're looking at a series of tumbledown shacks and trailers that declare, "You have completely left the Adirondack Park." You worry that you have left the Adirondack Park for good and, in your retirement, you will occupy one of these rural slums and get to know your neighbors. And resemble them. The road keeps curving between slums and a horse-rendering plant and an auto parts warehouse, and a wooden boat for sale that is set on a log crib now collapsing. When you were a child, the same wooden boat existed in the same vulnerable place—freshly painted white and blue, curtains in all three visible windows—and you asked your father why he would not buy it, and he said, "James, where would we put it?" You had no answer. The boat became more important than the official sign, as a marker of where you were. *In the park or out.* It made you cry then, and much more deeply now, years later, after the father who would not buy that boat, despite the begging, was long dead.

I own two properties in the Silver Lake area—one accessible by car, the other accessible only by boat. On the lake.

Property number one: I hear three sharp taps, then silence, then four more, accelerating, the sound of a woodpecker working its way into the trunk of a dying hemlock, the one that holds up the northeast corner of the tree house in which I sit. The tree house is a triangular "folly"—located dead center on the wilderness property I own, bought several years ago from a woman named Joan DeWitt.

"There's your *folly*," Cheryl, my former wife, said, the last time she visited my off-lake property, bouncing on that word, pleased with herself for having come up with it. "Must be a thousand dollars of wasted lumber and nails and shingles. And how many hours of labor?" And then she averted her eyes, still muttering about money. It wasn't her money. Nothing mine was ever hers—the way she wanted it. She had a couple million from winning the lottery. A million and a half. When she said, "A thousand dollars," she said it somewhat scornfully, as if she would not bend over to pick up an envelope with those very words written on it.

But that was not the way she talked about the property when I first showed it to her. "I love it," she said. "You have wild raspberries, an acre of them. How wonderful! We could pick and share with the locals. And the view of the mountain—"

"Hogback."

"Oh, *that*," she said. "I should have known. Well, at least the wretched fire tower is gone."

"Long ago," I said. "Erased." No need to dwell on her difficult past. And I was only a teenager in a Utica suburb when it happened.

"Let's look the other way," she said. "There are other mountains." Yes, other mountains, but the view was blocked by trees.

We rarely talked about her father. When we did, she would refer to him as Frank, as if he were a distant cousin, or completely unrelated. If I slipped up and referred to him as "Dad," she would roll her eyes and change the subject.

My folly should have collapsed during the winter. I feared the worst. Late April, the first thing I did when I drove north from the city, speeding past the ENTERING ADIRONDACK PARK sign, was head directly to my off-the-lake property and hike the two tenths of a mile from the driveway to the tree house. I was expecting a caved-in roof. *Intact*. I laughed, thinking how Cheryl might also have laughed. Dead leaves and woodpecker sawdust had blown into the crevices of the tree house, mice had knocked an empty water bottle from a shelf, had nibbled aluminum foil and processed it into a trail of aluminum turds. A bit of screen material flapped loose, easily fixed using the on-site rusty hammer and nails.

It is raining for the tenth straight day, and the top of my head is protected, although a direct wind could slap me in the face and send me back to my car. Not much to carry: a paperback trail guide, a quart of water, a ragged towel (left behind by a long-ago guest at my lake cabin, five miles south of here), a can of bug spray, a package of two-ply white Kleenex tissues. I have a persistent cold, and I've spent the past two days engaged in activities that will either distract me from my cold or make it radically worse. Like, sitting in an open-sided tree house in fifty-degree weather.

Property number two: Ten miles south of property number one, boat-access only (or a very difficult bush-whack). I was chopping wood for the fireplace in a north-facing and freezing-in-July waterfront cabin, on its near-island peninsula—for a guest who never showed up, never called to cancel. In the old days, pre-lottery, the guest could have been Cheryl. Could have been a friend, a relative, a former in-law.

And then I would have to get rid of these people, ferry them back to the "mainland," the unpaved and puddled lot where they had parked their cars. I'm coughing right now, thinking about such difficult crossings. Cheryl would say, "You need to talk to the town government about building a road *all the way* to your camp, James. It doesn't have to be paved. Just a road, two lanes wide. To end all this trouble with boats." *Your camp.*

"They'd have to extend the south shore road a quarter mile and fill in a major swamp. It would take an act of the New York State legislature."

"You've used that excuse before," she said.

"It would cost a million dollars."

"That one, too."

Once she told me she needed a pack of gum—she always chewed three sticks at a time, always spearmint—and I said, "Such an errand will cost five dollars' worth of gas, to the store and back," or, "You could row all the way, or hire someone to row you." We both had a good laugh. "You could bushwhack," I added.

"And then jog the rest of the way," she said. "I actually need the exercise."

I disagreed. She hadn't jogged much lately, but her thirty years as a high school gym teacher and track coach—now retired at fifty-five—had kept her in excellent shape. In our jogging days, our hiking days, I had trouble keeping up with her, always yelling, "Wait up!" Some forty years ago, she took second place in the New York State high school 10K run. She went to college on a track scholarship, SUNY Cortland. She was a member of the US Olympic team. Hurdles.

When she asked again about having a road built to our boat-access-only peninsula, I simply answered,

"Next summer," implying in her mind, I suppose, that the road would be built by then, but not meaning that at all. I meant, *We'll discuss it again next summer.*

"I picture a lovely road," she said. "Adding value to the property."

"True."

"Another piece of the paradise puzzle. This place could be perfect. Only a few tweaks."

Cheryl's father, when very old, left the Adirondack Park against his will, driven in a medi-cab by professionals to a place where he could be watched, if not rehabbed, by another set of dedicated professionals until he withered and died, disconnected from the wilderness that kept him active into his late eighties. Not everyone can stay in the Adirondacks through old age and death and burial. "What do you want?" people ask me, when I tell them I've been messing around on my wilderness acres, splitting firewood, digging up rocks, painting the outhouse, creating my own pond. "You want to *die* out there, where none of us can reach you? A tree could fall on you and it would be two weeks before we noticed you hadn't shown up for your morning latte or picked up your reserved *New York Times*." The outhouse is not the deal-killer; the deal-killer is the lack of cellphone coverage, a dead zone extending at least ten miles in every direction. I have no problem with isolation. My will states that I wish to be buried in the middle of this triangular patch of wilderness, which I am currently trying to clear for solar panels (and a rocket-flare launcher), and I will erect a cairn marking a rare soft spot in the earth where a small urn might be placed, but I cannot trust my relatives. In order to sell the property, they would make sure there were no bodies buried on it, among other issues, including the fact that the place lies completely off the grid—no water, no electricity, no cable—and it would take four or five utility poles to connect it to the fragile power line that, in turn, connects us to the city, to all cities, the power that fails in every storm.

So who needs it? In a few minutes I will hike down the hill to the driveway and get in my car and drive to the coffee shop. Espresso, tea, baked goods. Although it's past lunchtime, I'll ask for a breakfast burrito (potatoes, egg, cheese). I need cooked food on a day like this.

One time Cheryl's father called from the nursing home—I had to believe he was in the nursing home, not out in the cold and rainy world, as he claimed to be—and he said, "James, I hitched a ride as far as Demarests, as far as they go. You have to come get me. I'm standing here at the pay phone and it's gonna rain bobcats and coyotes any minute now. They locked the goddamn door on me. I can't get in!" Demarests was the tavern northwest of Silver Lake where the old man used to run a tab, which he paid up maybe twice a year, if he paid up at all. By the time of his phone call, the tavern had gone out of business, the tiny windows boarded up, this dark log cabin with a caved-in roof and a pond for a parking lot. Even the Mountain Lakes Realty FOR SALE sign had been chopped in two.

In his mind the old man had never left the Adirondacks.

"James," he said. His daughter and I had been divorced for a year. Why, then, would he be calling me? Only if he had somehow hitched a ride to Demarests could he logically be calling me for a ride back to his wilderness double-wide. Which he would have done decades ago, impaired by drink, or carless.

"Where *are* you, Dad?"

"I told you. And I'm standing in the goddamn rain because you can't get off your lazy ass and pick me up."

"If you really *are* at Demarests, it means I have to fire up the motorboat and ride to my car and then drive another eight miles. Which could take an hour."

"I'm melting here," he said. "They stole my hat. I'll be all gone in an hour. A pillar of salt."

"What?"

"You need to have your earwax cleaned out, James. You keep saying 'what?' Aren't I talking loud enough for you?"

"You're plenty loud, but quite frankly I don't believe you're anywhere near Demarests."

"What good are you then?" He coughed—a long, deep cough, enough to change the atmospheric pressure, even in the room where I paced, its lakeside windows shut against the rain.

After the coughing had cleared, I said, "I don't hear any highway noise."

"Why would you? It's the end of the world out here. I can't hear one frog peeping. This joint used to hop, all summer. Old Demarest would bring the girls up from Utica and have a dozen of them prancing around on the stage, bare naked, live music, the cops busting down the front door while we all ran out the back into the woods. You really missed something, James. You and Cheryl. Too much hiking's not good for the soul."

"She stopped hiking. We're not together."

"Not one frog peeping," he said.

I told him I could hear music in the background, upbeat, Lawrence Welk, which should have been enough to prove that I knew where he was. Then I added, "It's hardly the kind of music cops get excited about." Nursing home music—a sedative, which, in his case, had no effect.

"You better get your ears checked," he said with a chuckle. "You're not as young as you used to be."

"I know."

"Running up and down the mountain in one breath. You still doing that?"

"Not as much." Then I heard the rain, through the phone. I believed it was rain, a hard rain. "You said you were standing out in the rain with no hat?"

"Nothing is where it's supposed to be," he said.

The gist of the story is that we kept talking, and my father-in-law had me in a panic. *Hatless, in the rain, eighty-eight years old.* I hung up in the middle of a sentence about an overnight camping trip we might share (only if I came and got him before he melted). I immediately jumped in the damn utility boat without wiping down the seat and made it to the Point during a cloudburst, then changed into dry clothes in my car—I always kept dry clothes in my car—and drove barefoot to Demarests, where, of course, there was no pay phone, no phone of any kind, no old man looking for a ride, only a yellow sign asking the public to "report any vandalism to the county sheriff," and so I turned around and drove south, out of the Adirondacks, past the LEAVING sign and the sad, sad crumbling wooden boat, down into the foothills, and the small dying cities, to the place where my father-in-law was now supposed to be a resident—a low-rise, cement-block nursing facility with three-foot-square windows, one per room, hard to see out of and facing away from the mountains he loved. I put on my socks and boots and walked into the place. When I asked the on-duty supervisor about my father-in-law, she said, "He never leaves the building. We have excursions to church, to the mall, to museums, movies. He never goes." He was asleep in his room.

When was the last time Cheryl checked on him? Did they even talk on the phone? It might have been too painful for her.

Cheryl took a different route when she left. I followed her in my car. At first, it seemed she was pointing her Lexus toward the center of the Adirondacks—reasonable, for if you're leaving paradise, you might want to take a close look at it.

A strange discovery: the public airport at Piseco Lake does not appear on my 1993 map of the area, one inch to the mile, fully contoured. What relevance would an airport have to the users of this map? It might repel them. Who, for example, would fly in at Piseco and then begin hiking the Northville-Placid Trail at its midpoint? In our separate and unequal vehicles, Cheryl and I had been driving north from Silver Lake on a two-lane state highway with no services, no power line, only a scattering of shacks along the river, hunting camps, and one demented hitchhiker, hatless in the rain, whom I splashed while laughing derisively. I kept my distance from Cheryl. I stayed twenty car lengths back, with another vehicle between us, like a decoy, a black minivan with tinted windows. "Thanks for giving me cover, bud," I said out loud. At one point, though, a great blue heron got in front of me, flying six feet above the pavement. I honked at the damn thing—it was only going twenty—and the bird shifted over to the left lane so I could pass. As I passed the bird, I gave him a look. He looked at me. He had a head like a vulture, an ugly scowling head, like he was pissed at me for honking. *For existing in his park, for owning two different pieces of property, both of which he wished to lay claim to.* I did fifty on the tight curves and caught up with the minivan, which turned west at the T-intersection. The Lexus turned east. I followed, mystified. Did we discuss this?

"I'm leaving," she had told me the same morning, tossing a banana peel into the woods, a recycling gesture, and only a gesture, as she had customarily (until that morning) sealed everything in Hefty bags and arranged them on the dock to be hauled away by boat and then by car to the transfer station. One may imagine the awkwardness of the boat ride we shared following the announcement that she was leaving—literally leaving, and also what is meant on another level by the trite phrase *I'm leaving you.* The loud motor helped, creating a buffer between us. The common courtesies of tying up at the mainland dock were observed. Please and thank you. We hauled her stuff out of the boat, wiped the dew off our car windows, and started our engines. I headed toward the coffee shop, Cheryl tailgating me those three miles. We stood in line for our coffee as if nothing had happened. We chatted with Cheryl's cousin Jayne, who always asked about the boat ride over: Bumpy? Windy? Did you get wet? Are you *cold*? Good day for a *large* coffee. One shot or two?

I then sat at the red picnic table, the loon-counting table—the temperature was sixty degrees with a windchill—and warmed myself briefly by transferring the coffee cup from one hand to the other. My wife took her cinnamon bun to her car and began driving one-handed—north, nibbling. I had to follow. What the hell? North? *Leaving the Adirondacks means going south.*

Near the end of her leaving, we passed the sign for the Episcopal Church (nine miles ahead) and did the eight-mile stretch of state highway south of Piseco Lake, then turned left at Rudeston, on the county road that eventually connects to the public campsites along the north shore. I almost missed the final turn, thinking, *Picnic at Little Sand Point*. Which means she's not leaving. Then, *Airport*? Yes, there it was, a real airport, angling northeast and thus parallel to all the glaciated lakes, a full runway, with lights, a modern terminal, and a weather station with a red windsock and a children's playground, six or seven cars parked in a paved lot, Infinitis and Outbacks.

It was a secret airport, like the one behind Mount Rushmore in Hitchcock's *North by Northwest*. Cheryl pulled into a spot, waited a minute, then got out, no cinnamon bun. None available in the terminal. She had changed into clogs and, somehow, a mid-calf skirt. She began walking toward the runway and the small plane parked there, propellers already spinning. She was pulling two large suitcases I'd never seen before. They might have been stashed in her car, weeks ago. A plane door opened and Cheryl climbed in. Briefly, I saw a short-sleeved arm reach out to help her. They taxied, two heads in silhouette.

Flying lessons? She could afford them. I finished my coffee and filled my mouth with peppermint gum. Absurd thoughts came to mind: Why fly out of here? Why not run all the way? You're still in great shape. You used to tell me about a fantasy—how, when you were young, you believed the best way out of Lost River was to tighten your shoelaces and run, never look back.

The plane took off, clearing the trees with Cheryl aboard, and no sign for leaving the park in evidence, no banner flapping behind and spelling out those words. She had found a new way to leave. I was stuck there, and if I was miserable, it had nothing to do with my inability to leave, nor the crumbling infrastructure of my Adirondack world, the diminishing connections with relatives and friends, the two minutes of conversation that accompanied my morning cup of coffee and cinnamon scone. "Oh, you're spending more time up at your tree house now," Cousin Jayne might say in the future, regarding a place she'd never visited. "No electricity? An outhouse? All by yourself? Way too primitive for me." It had nothing to do with that. Such comments would make me smile.

I shielded my eyes as Cheryl's plane disappeared into the refracted sun. She would look down from several thousand feet, I hoped, and feel a measure of understanding toward me—despite the bad geography we had shared—finally seeing the land as a map, which it always is when you're not on it, when you've left it behind and revisit only by virtue of two-dimensional representations and fuzzy satellite pictures that cannot tell whether the tree house has fallen, nor who, in particular, might be standing by the edge of the road during a cloudburst, looking for a way in or out.

Afterword

Many of these stories are anchored by an Adirondack general store—a place that defines the local community. It is the place where the loon counters gather after counting the loons on the local lakes. It is the place where, owing to bad cell coverage, people must communicate with each other—sometimes face-to-face, sometimes by posting notices on the bulletin board. A place of employment, past and present. The woman who owns and runs the store knows all, but does not necessarily *tell* all. Max, the local boat mechanic and boat dealer, thinks that he knows everyone, but he's too young. Occasionally, the fictional town of Silver Lake overlaps with the real Adirondacks, but more often it resists assimilation. It remains a secret place, very much resembling other Adirondack towns, but disconnected to the extent that it would be a wild guess to try to pinpoint it on the map.

Previous versions of the following stories were published in *Blueline*: "North of Cooperstown" (vol. 24, 2003), "The Hiker" (vol. 33, 2012), "Counting Loons" (vol. 35, 2014), "Leaving Adirondack Park" (vol. 39, 2018), "Vanishing Point" (originally published as "Violinist," vol. 44, 2023), "Adirondack Tenors" (vol. 45, 2024), and "Silver Creek" (vol. 46, 2025).

Roger Sheffer has published three collections of fiction: *Lost River* (Night Tree Press, 1988), *Borrowed Voices* (New Rivers Press, 1990), and *Music of the Inner Lakes* (New Rivers Press, 1999). He has won several national short story contests, and his stories have appeared in many magazines, including *Blueline*, *The Missouri Review*, *Third Coast*, *Arts and Letters*, and *Adirondack Life*. He taught writing and literature at Minnesota State University, Mankato, from 1980 to 2016.